DEATH DRIVES AN AUDI

Kristian Bang Foss (b. 1977) is a graduate of the Danish Writers' School. He made his debut in 2004 with *The Fish Window*, and his second novel, *The Storm Of '99* (2008), received widespread critical acclaim. Bang Foss became an international success with his third novel, *Death Drives an Audi*, which received the European Union Prize for Literature in 2013 and has thus far been published in nineteen countries.

Caroline Waight is an award-winning literary translator working from Danish and German. She has translated a wide range of fiction and non-fiction, with recent publications including *The Invention of Ana*, *The Chestnut Man* and *The Gravediggers*. She worked in publishing before becoming a full-time literary translator. She now lives and works in London.

DEATH DRIVES AN AUDI

KRISTIAN BANG FOSS

TRANSLATED BY CAROLINE WAIGHT

Parthian, Cardigan SA43 1ED
www.parthianbooks.com
First published in Great Britain by Parthian
Originally published in Denmark as *Døden kører
Audi* by Gyldendal in 2012
© Kristian Bang Foss 2012
English translation © Caroline Waight 2020
All Rights Reserved
ISBN 978-1-912681-32-7
eISBN 978-1-913640-37-8
Cover design and typesetting by Syncopated
Pandemonium
Cover illustration by Mathis Burmeister
Printed and bound by 4Edge in the UK
Published with the financial support of the Welsh
Books Council. The publisher would also like to
thank the Danish Arts Foundation for support
towards the translation and publication of this book.
Co-funded by the Creative Europe Programme of
the European Union

British Library Cataloguing in Publication Data
A cataloguing record for this book is available from
the British Library.

Death Drives an Audi

It started out so straightforward. I lived in a flat in Copenhagen with Sara and Amalie, and if I got up from the sofa in the evening when we were sitting in front of the TV after Amalie had gone to bed, Sara would say, *What are you doing?* Even in the middle of the night if I got up to pee, she'd say, *What are you doing?* I'd say, *Going for a pee*, I'd say, *To check on Amalie*, I'd say, *To make some coffee*, I'd say, *For a walk.*

I walked a lot. Getting out of the apartment for a bit was how I kept my weight down. But then from time to time people began to look. I think I was becoming part of the scenery, like Two-Kroner Man, Singer Søren or one of the others wandering the streets, so I walked a little less. But it was never more than a month before I started getting pudgy again, couldn't even see my own pubic hair when I stood under the shower, and I resumed my walks.

"You and your eternal walks," said Sara. It annoyed her, my hankering to be outside. We'd begun to get on each other's nerves, and not just sometimes. It was a permanent state of irritation, and it was too soon to be getting on each other's nerves permanently, because Amalie was only four and we'd only just bought the flat.

Amalie wasn't my daughter. Her so-called biological dad got some kind of psychosis and was never really the same after that. He's a Hare Krishna now. I saw him once: he came dancing down the street in orange robes with the other Krishnas, playing the tambourine. He gave me a little cake. I didn't fancy eating it. I never told Sara I'd seen him. Don't ask me why not – I mean, it wasn't wrong, me seeing him and getting the cake – but we just never really talked about him. Now and again I caught myself thinking, I hope it's not genetic. In a way it would have been better if I was Amalie's real dad, but you can't think like that, of course, because otherwise there would be no Amalie. See? That's what I mean – so as a rule I didn't think about it much. Amalie called me Dad.

That day I'd gone downstairs to eat a roast pork sandwich and got back to the office at half twelve. I had a few hours to turn a proposal into a campaign, which we were supposed to present to the client later that afternoon. Håkon, who hated me for some reason, knew I was screwed, and he kept circling me with a malicious smile, trying to distract me.

"How's it going with the presentation?"

"It's going great, Håkon."

"Super. I'm looking forward to hearing what you've come up with."

"I'm sure you are."

Håkon sat down at his desk and began to click his pen. Click-click, click-click, click-click. I think I know, by the way, why he hated me. He hated me because he'd ended up getting plastered and telling me something at the office Christmas lunch a few years earlier. Something intimate. I don't remember what it was; all I remember is that he put his face up close to mine, his eyes small and wet behind his office glasses. The fact that he'd left himself exposed, that he thought I had something on him, that I knew he had a weak spot somewhere; that made him hate me. Unfortunate, but that was that. Click-click, click-click, click-click. So this was his present contribution to the cosy atmosphere, the clicking.

"Håkon, would you mind not clicking that pen?"

"Is it bothering you?"

"Yes."

"Sorry – I just think so much better when I click."

Håkon stopped. To be on the safe side, I took out my iPod, stuffed the earbuds into my ears and switched on Bruce Springsteen's *Nebraska*. Then my phone went. Sara, asking if I'd remembered I was supposed to pick Amalie up early from kindergarten at one o'clock. I lied and said I *had* remembered, that I was on my way. I'd have to bank on coming up with an idea on the way to the kindergarten, then bring Amalie back to the office with me for a couple of hours.

The reason the kindergarten had to close was that the entire staff of teachers were going for emergency counselling with an emergency counsellor at the big hospital, because there had been some criticism of their accounting in the media. It was a really tangled affair that would have delighted me if it hadn't been so inconvenient.

I took the car up to the kindergarten, arriving five minutes late. One of the teachers was crying on a three-legged stool while another comforted her by patting her shoulder, eyeing me accusingly. Over in the corner, Amalie was fighting with another girl over a Hans Bellmer-like doll with a missing arm.

The girl wrenched the doll out of Amalie's hand. Its remaining arm poked out into the air like it was Sieg-Heiling. She celebrated her victory by settling down to gnaw on the doll's head. I picked up Amalie and kissed her, grabbed her stuff, then said goodbye to the crying and comforting teachers and returned to the car.

Back at the office with Amalie, I found a notepad and some felt tip pens and put her next to me, leaving her to draw. Maybe she could help Dad draw some nice pictures for the ad? Håkon was nowhere to be seen.

It was only a small task. Some cultural entrepreneur had got a load of money from the local authority to organise a fair for cross-cultural art in the Meatpacking District. All I had to contribute was a poster advertising the thing, but I was drawing a total blank. I couldn't put aside my antipathy to his phony, well-meaning event. I'd met the guy once, and his shifty gaze, his inability to make eye contact, had given me the shivers. Amalie had spread her finished drawings over the table and was now working on a new one. The sun in the top right corner was being given rays.

The art fair was called Cross Purposes. A silly idea popped into my head. Googling "eating spaghetti", I found a photo of a businessman slurping up a piece of spaghetti between his lips. It was perfect. After a bit more googling I found a picture of a Sikh blowing a kiss. I downloaded both pictures, checked the resolution was decent, and set to work. The result was a picture of a white businessman and an Indian in a turban, each sucking their respective ends of a string of spaghetti, like *Lady and the Tramp*. A stock photo would have been better, but there was no point reaching for the stars. All I could do now was hope the guy bought it. I didn't give a shit about the image rights. They were from an American and Italian website, and the likelihood that what I'd done would be discovered was minimal.

I also got the idea to print a number of T-shirts with the text CROSS PURPOSES – ART HAS NO HOMELAND, which would be handed out among the city's homeless. The homeless were the new Black right now among the "creative classes". It was hip to look like a homeless person, to know a homeless person or be connected to one.

The organiser lapped it up. He loved the provocative element and wasn't capable of recognising it as hack work. Håkon was about to die of apoplexy. I'd asked him to look after Amalie during the presentation, and when I came out and said we'd sold it, his face lit up with a smile so false that she began to cry. I took the rest of the day off and drove home with Amalie.

On the way we bought stuff for dinner and cooked together until Sara came home. It turned out to be an exceptionally good evening, and after dinner and a bedtime story for Amalie I sat down in front of the TV with a glass of red wine, well pleased.

It took a month for the hammer to fall. The fat businessman in the photo turned out not to be a businessman at all, but the head of some kind of league of Italian fascists. It was a journalist who recognised him. A representative from the Danish–Indian Friendship Association complained, demanding public apologies from all and sundry. The apparatchik flipped out. The poster had knocked the wind out of his event and its positive, edifying image. I asked why all art had to be good and told him he should be happy with all the free PR, but he didn't buy it. Then on top of everything else, by some crazy coincidence the Italian fascist found out about the frankly rather insignificant case up north and allied himself with the photographer who owned the copyright to the image, taking the agency to court.

This was mid-2008, and the crisis had begun. Every job in the industry was hanging by a thread, so for my boss this was a heaven-sent opportunity to fire another man. I had to close my MacBook and say goodbye to the others at the office. Håkon acted all grief-stricken. I suspected he'd been busy behind the scenes during the shitstorm.

At first I didn't take it all that hard.

I sent off applications and managed to score a few interviews, but I was closer to forty than thirty, and that's old in the advertising world. In any case, the interviews seemed to have been arranged primarily because ritual humiliation pleased the interviewer, rather than because there was a real chance of a job. I became another over-educated guy on benefits, and after a while I gave up sending off applications. I turned up at a white office in a public building where they tried to motivate me, and I played along, thinking it was my civic duty to make sure they had something to get their teeth into.

I stopped going for walks. They weren't fun anymore; I had nothing to think about as I walked. No nuts to crack. Now I either lay on the sofa or trundled around the flat. On the days Sara took Amalie to kindergarten, I didn't get dressed. I could feel Sara getting irritated coming home to someone still in a dressing gown, so I made sure to put on clothes before she got back, but after a while that routine broke down too. Then there were only the fridge and the sofa left. I started eating more. I was hungry almost all the time. Sometimes I'd wake up in the night, thinking about the leftover ham salad in the darkness of the refrigerator, and I'd get out of bed and eat standing up, gulping silky-smooth juice out of the carton. At twelve I usually opened my first can of beer, then there was wine for dinner and whiskey in the evening. It was only a phase, I told myself; right now there was no work, there was no reason to look. But it would get better in a year or so, when the economy turned, and I had to pass the time somehow till then. I threw out the empty cans before Sara came home. I don't know if she noticed that I stank of beer and was already tipsy by dinner time, but either way she didn't say anything.

One day when I'd started early and had just finished off the first six-pack, squeezing the cans flat and carrying them down to the bins, Sara rang and asked me to pick up Amalie. She was working overtime.

I borrowed Sara's bike, which was the only thing that had a child seat. Amalie chatted away in her seat as I cycled home through the city, answering yes and no and asking the occasional question. The sky was blue with a sun, like one of Amalie's drawings. A family was packing the car for a trip to the beach. Seized by the atmosphere, I turned my head to ask, *Why don't we buy some vanilla ice cream and Sprite?*, but the front wheel bumped the curb. My feet flew off the pedals, I lost control of the bike and we fell.

Luckily, it's a milk tooth, they said at A&E. I was sitting there with Amalie's blood on my crumpled shirt. I myself was unscathed.

Over the next week I couldn't bear to see Amalie smile. When we ate dinner, I had to take a big gulp of red wine every time I saw the gap where the front tooth should have been. She herself took it like a champ. It was more Sara who was upset, and after a week it was over. I was lying on the sofa, eating and drinking, when she dumped me. The TV was on in the background.

I moved in temporarily with my friend Stanley. I sent group emails and put ads online and wrote status updates on Facebook to find a flat as quickly as possible. A couple of nights I called Sara, but she didn't answer. I slept on Stanley's sofa. During the day I cleaned up a bit and emptied the dishwasher – something to say thanks for my spot on the couch. Stanley didn't seem to mind me being there. The weekend came, and we went into town. Stanley was a commercial lawyer, and they'd won a case at work, and he said we should celebrate. You need to get out a bit, he said. We ended up at a concept bar in the city centre. The group next to us were American, and when they started irritating us enormously, and it turned out the college boy at the end of the table was having a birthday, we improvised the following birthday song:

How old are you now?
How old are you now?
You'll get cancer in the asshole
And then you will die

I couldn't stop bawling with laughter. Satisfied with our own wit, we left the bar and went home. I flopped onto the sofa. Stanley sat on the chair next to me. We talked politics, and we couldn't agree on who we hated most: the so-called right wing, the so-called left wing or the so-called centre parties. Stanley fetched a bottle of whiskey from the cupboard and poured us glasses, giving a little monologue about single malt. We talked about Sara and Amalie. Then suddenly Stanley began to cry and say he'd worn two pairs of trousers at once for ages because he was worried about having such thin legs.

We woke up the next day with a hangover. I made bacon and fried eggs. Stanley ate a quarter of the white and poked a hole in the yolk and sat staring at what flowed out. On Sunday I was offered a one-room flat in Sydhavnen and accepted straight away. Stanley and another friend helped me move my things out there. Sara wasn't home when we picked them up. I bought a bottle of Highland Park for Stanley as thanks for letting me borrow his sofa.

Six months passed in the Sydhavnen flat. I put on fifteen kilos. After repeatedly failing to show up at meetings at the unemployment office because of a hangover, or simply because the days were flowing into one and the hours were turned on their head, I was barred and the money stopped coming. Goodbye and thank you. This was the age of night-time television. Night-time television – there's something special about watching TV at night during the week. When everything is quiet in the flat and it's approaching three a.m., and you flick from an ice hockey match to the shopping channel to an American series, and one by one the channels fall away, and the screen flickers into grey. You go over to the window and stare out at the house fronts, and most windows are dark. This is where the healthy people with jobs live, where they sleep the working man's good and natural sleep. But other windows are still lit. Not with the yellowish-orange glow of candles, but with the radiance of night-time TV: the cold blue light of a machine that's been on since dinner. Or the jerky flash of a porn film – porn light, I called it; you can see it in the rhythmic shifting of the light, the flesh-coloured glow that pulses behind the curtain. I didn't dare switch off the TV until I was anaesthetised with tiredness and the transition didn't seem as abrupt on the senses, the silence that appeared wasn't so violent, because I was already on my way into sleep.

The envelopes of reminders and flyers accumulated in the hall. Rubbish and empty bottles accumulated in bags by the kitchen door. Dirty dishes accumulated on the kitchen table. Fat accumulated beneath the skin. Everything piled up and accumulated except money. My debit card was frozen. One day I was at the supermarket about to pay, and I had to leave the goods and go. I borrowed from my friends; I owed Stanley ten thousand kroner.

But one day it wouldn't fly anymore. Flabby and hung-over, I took the train west and got off at Stentofte Station. I was going to a job interview.

I'd borrowed another five thousand from Stanley to pay the rent, and he'd twisted my arm and made me promise I would get a job. Any job. I said it was impossible, we were in a financial crisis. He said that if you're not fussy there's always something: McDonald's, 7-Eleven, cleaning. "It'll be good for you," he laughed. "You need to get out of that cave."

He even called and woke me in the morning to be sure I got up in time. I sang Jodle Birge's "Real

Friends" in a drowsy, bitter voice down the line and hung up, but I got up and got dressed and got myself down to Dybbølsbro Station. The job was as a carer for the disabled.

I'd never been to Stentofte before, and when I disembarked at the station I understood why. If Hieronymus Bosch or Bruegel had lived in 2008, they wouldn't have painted pictures of harlots being raped by skeletons and men tumbling shrieking into the seething fat of Satan's frying pan, armies of the dead pouring forth and laying waste to everything; no, they'd have painted Stentofte's concrete. If you think hell doesn't exist, then get onto the B line and ride it all the way to Stentofte.

Of course, I'd ridden through it on the train on the way to Jutland. I'd seen the postmodern monstrosity of a station building from the carriage as the train passed; I'd seen the Pedestal of Joy sculpture outside Stentofte Town Hall, towering above the station building, but I'd never been on the platform. I set off for the escalators and rode up to the main hall. A few commuters were on their way to work, a shabby individual was sleeping on a bench and a small group of young men were hanging out at the top of the escalators, so you had no choice but to pass close by them. Not that they did anything to anyone – they just stood there – but somehow they managed to instil fear in the passers-by. One of them tossed a cigarette butt onto the ground behind me. Another hawked loudly and spat on the floor.

Outside I looked at a page from an old street atlas,

which I'd ripped out and stuffed into my pocket. I was supposed to go right, in the opposite direction from the Pedestal of Joy, which towered like a lighthouse, its cheerful colours underscoring the general dreariness and making the whole thing even worse.

There was a Chinese restaurant on the corner of the station building. It had long since gone bust, the windows were painted white, but there was a thin dog barking outside like it wanted to be let in. Then the station building stopped, and there was a patch of undeveloped land. The idea had probably been that housing blocks would shoot up here once the station was finished, but that hadn't happened. Beyond the area of brownfield was a large, crowded road, and on the other side of the road was a day-care centre and a football pitch surrounded by a tall wire fence, and behind the football pitch were the housing blocks. This was where Waldemar lived.

They say the perfect labyrinth consists of as many identical modules as possible, and it wasn't long before I was wandering, now late, among the interchangeable grey concrete buildings, looking at the numbers above the red and blue doors, which seemed to change utterly at random. I reached a playground I thought I'd already passed, then realised there were the remains of a fire on the slide that I didn't recognise. It had to be a different playground. Elsewhere the houses slid further apart, eventually giving way to a large plane of grass. I crossed. It reeked of dog shit. It was now a few minutes past nine, and I decided to go back home if I hadn't found number 36 in block 3A before ten minutes had passed. But my chances of going home were instantly scuppered, because of course 3A turned out to be the block at the end of the grass.

Waldemar lived in the flat on the left. In the flat on the right the blinds were drawn, but I could see someone adjust them slightly at the corner, the better to observe. The rectangular plastic doorbell seemed dead the first time I pressed it, but after I'd coaxed and manoeuvred it a bit, the lock buzzed and I was let inside.

As I waited in the stairwell, I could hear Waldemar rattling with bolts and security chains behind the door. I was sure the neighbour was watching me through the spyhole. Then the door opened.

Waldemar was short. Not so short you'd call him a dwarf, but short enough that I was looking over his head into thin air when the door opened. Angling my gaze down a little, I found his face: vampire-white skin with a colony of large pimples on his brow; green eyes magnified by a pair of very powerful black-framed glasses. His hair was shoulder-length – on the top of his head it lay flat, but as it grew away from the skull it started twisting into small black curls. His parting reminded me of a gash in a blackout curtain, where a cold light shone through. Making him seem even shorter was his poor posture, which bordered on the hunchbacked. He invited me inside.

Two cups and a Thermos jug were laid out on

a coffee table in the living room. The space was remarkably impersonal – I mean, I'm not the type of person who's into giving things a *personal* stamp, but the décor was somehow uncanny. It reminded me of a hospital waiting room.

"I've made real coffee," he said.

We sat down by the table.

Waldemar told me all about his diseases and syndromes. He was a walking textbook of rare and unpleasant ailments, suffering from a countless array of things I'd have killed to avoid. A documentary I'd seen during one of my night-time TV sessions popped into my head. It was about a woman who'd been struck six times by lightning. There was the same unreasonableness at work here.

He had a muscle disorder that meant he couldn't move much without getting tired, and a heart defect the doctors had carved him up twice in an attempt to repair, but the bottom line was that his heart was unlikely to last that many more years. In fact, the doctors considered it unnatural that he wasn't dead yet. Afterwards the thought came to me that Waldemar must have had superhuman physical toughness and endurance to survive even a single day with all the illnesses nature had heaped upon him. There was another one that had impeded his growth, but I'm certain that if the growth-impeding syndrome hadn't intervened he would have been a giant, at least two metres tall; if he hadn't had this muscular disorder he'd have been monstrously strong; and if he hadn't lived his entire life in a wasteland of stupidity, I don't think there would have been any limit to what he might have accomplished. But his existence was devoid of any hint of inspiration, and his everyday life was spent navigating between zones of human callousness and bureaucratic condescension. He was also the stubbornest person I'd ever met, and above all I think it was his enormous stubbornness that kept his tatter of a heart still beating.

Waldemar didn't usually talk that much about his disorders, I discovered later, but he probably felt it was part of the job description. Maybe I was supposed to know it was possible he would fall down dead while I was at work.

He ferried himself around in a motorised wheelchair, and found it hard to manage even the simplest things at home without becoming utterly shattered. For this reason the local authority had given him money to employ a carer to come over thirty-seven hours a week and help with practical stuff. His current carer had resigned, so he needed to find a new one. He also told me he was twenty-two years old, and that his parents lived in another block at the opposite end of Stentofte.

I told him a bit about myself, most of it lies and pseudo-truths.

Later that day, as I sat at home in my flat in Sydhavnen, he called and said I'd got the job. I was starting the next day. I hung up and stared into space.

That evening I phoned Sara. She still wasn't picking up the phone. Then, for the first time in ages, I took a walk. I hoped some fresh air would help me fall asleep. The thought of Stentofte gave me a feeling of physical distaste. But maybe it would be better once spring had properly arrived – it was still only March.

When I showed up the next morning for my first day of work, Waldemar said we had to clean the bathroom, and that it would take an hour. He stood in the doorway and watched. When he got tired of standing, he sat in the living room and rested for a bit. His knack for appearing soundlessly in the doorway meant it always took me a while to realise I was being watched.

The toilet was already clean, so that bit didn't take much effort. It could have been much worse, I thought, when I was finished. Adult diapers or something. This was child's play. Then we sat staring into space for an hour. Waldemar called it resting. I made us a cup of coffee. I couldn't figure out how I was supposed to act – how much I should do myself and how much I should leave to him. "Is there anything else we need to get done?" I said when the inactivity was starting to get on my nerves.

"There's loads," said Waldemar. Then he got up and fetched a block of yellow Post-it notes from the kitchen table. That turned out to be one of his things: the reminder notes he always wrote, as though he had a thousand things to remember. It said: "Peg".

The peg was the project of the day. Outside in the hallway there were two pegs: one where Waldemar hung the jacket he was using – currently a green parka – and beside it an identical peg with the word "carer" written on a wooden sign above it. Waldemar's peg had come loose. It was this loose peg that was our hero; this loose peg that was to save us throughout the day.

"I think I'd like a new one," he said, after we'd gone into the hallway and stared at the pegs. The screw at the top had lost its hold on the wall, and a bit of plaster had crumbled out. It was lying on the floor.

"Why don't we just screw the old one back into place?" I asked, like the idiot I was.

Waldemar ignored me and looked annoyed.

"Now that the old one is broken, I think I'd like a new one. We'll probably need a trip down to MegaMetropolis. I'll just have a bath first."

Waldemar had a bath. Afterwards he was completely white and had to rest for a while before we made it out the door.

"Will you sweep the hallway?" he asked me.

"But we'll make a mess again when the new peg goes up," I said. I still hadn't learned – it was only my first day, after all.

"The dustpan and brush are in the wardrobe," said Waldemar.

I swept the plaster into the dustpan. No matter how

much I swept, there was always a vanishingly thin strip left that wouldn't cooperate, so I went out and grabbed a piece of kitchen roll, moistened it under the tap, then sopped up the last bits of plaster. As I closed the wardrobe after putting the dustpan and brush back into place, fresh plaster drifted down from the screw hole.

MegaMetropolis was located where the motorway trimmed Stentofte. We crossed through the estate. Waldemar rode in his motorised wheelchair, and I walked beside him. Satellite dishes hung from the balconies, all staring at the same grey point in the sky. There was a massive blanket of dark clouds, which looked like they were resting on top of the high-rise blocks.

We moved among the blocks down a system of pathways, across a pedestrian bridge above a cycle path and then down an underpass beneath a road roaring with traffic. MegaMetropolis hove into view as we emerged. At first I underestimated its size: it turned out to be colossal, growing only gradually as we walked across the empty car park – like approaching a mountain.

MegaMetropolis consisted of four floors of businesses renting space. Many of them, however, were closed. It was clear that MegaMetropolis's glory days were already behind it. There was an atmosphere of protracted death. We trundled around the mall, looking into windows. At the bottom was a hardware store, where Waldemar bought two pegs, a packet of screws and some Rawlplugs.

We left the shop. Near the exit, at the corner of MegaMetropolis, was an Aldi.

"Let's just pop into Aldi," said Waldemar, "and see if they've got any offers on."

It was the moment I heard Waldemar talk about popping into Aldi that I landed with a crash. I'd been in freefall for a year. It was a culture shock, plain and simple. It goes without saying that I'd shopped at Netto. But from Netto there was still a way back – Netto is a place everybody knows, it's just a place to do your shopping on the cheap, but Aldi is something else altogether. It's hopelessness incarnate. The sausages in Aldi's freezers were pig's guts stuffed with a grey slurry of desperation and fear; the pork roulade was sliced sorrow; the cashier was a portrait of suicide.

A year ago I'd been sitting in the offices of the advertising agency, and now I was standing here with Waldemar among the chilled-food cabinets, which glowed and smoked with frost, in Aldi. Both the agency and Aldi were the products of a dying civilisation that had elevated lies to its highest ideal, and I had travelled from one end to the other. They were surprisingly different and frighteningly alike. Above one of the freezers hung a sign with a picture of a happy chicken, flapping its wings and announcing in a speech bubble: OUR PRICES ARE CHEEP!

An Asian woman was filling a shopping trolley with reduced-price chicken. The vapour played around them as they were lifted out of the cabinet.

"Let's check out that chicken," said Waldemar.

An old lady with a rollator was approaching at the same time as us. She had her little dog tethered to the frame. It wanted to go in the other direction and was pulling her off-course, so she was constantly having to correct.

Waldemar was trundling slowly in the wheelchair, but when he saw what was happening he accelerated with the little joystick to grab a chicken.

The woman put yet another chicken in her trolley, and when she saw there were other people approaching out of the corner of her eye, she leant all the way into the freezer and shovelled three of them into her arms.

Waldemar and the pensioner and I reached the freezer at the same time. All the chicken was gone. The pensioner stared into the empty freezer to show she was interested in one of the chickens the woman with the trolley still had in her arms.

She ignored us, threw the chickens into the trolley and rolled away.

"You put those chickens back!" someone yelled. It was a fat man in a leather jacket and sweatpants, hurrying across from the dairy aisle, where he'd left his trolley. His upper body swung so that his arms waggled as he walked.

The Asian woman acted like she didn't hear and bustled off with her trolley, but at the end of the aisle between the two long refrigerated counters an Aldi employee appeared. Despite his listless and indifferent attitude, he had decided to intervene. Planting himself between the freezers, he blocked her path, holding up four fingers.

"Four chickens per customer," he said. "Put the rest back. Now we've advertised them they need to last, or I'll be getting crap about it for the rest of the day."

She stopped the trolley.

"Put them back . . . Now!" said the man with the leather jacket and the swinging arms. "You can't just stand there pretending you don't understand what we're saying."

She took a step back from the trolley and threw up her hands in a gesture of resignation, but the man didn't stop. When he passed the dog, it gave an ear-splitting bark and leapt forward, sinking its teeth into his trouser leg. He tried to keep going with the dog and the rollator dangling behind him, lost his balance and stumbled, but stayed upright for another few steps by doing a few swimming strokes with his arms in the air. When he fell, he was close enough to the shopping trolley to grab the handle. Rearing up under his weight, it rolled away from him on its back wheels, until he was clinging on, fully outstretched in an arc, with the tips of his toes on the floor and his hands on the handle. Then the trolley flew all the way up onto its rear end, slamming first his belly then his face into the floor, and he ended up lying with his arms out straight, chickens raining down as though from the back of a truck. The dog let go of his trouser leg and ran away. During the yoga-esque fall we could hear his spine making cracking sounds. Once he was on the floor and all the chickens had stopped rolling, he groaned softly, and a puddle spread beneath him and his sweatpants grew wet: he was emptying his bladder like an animal being put to sleep.

The dog ran up and sniffed the puddle, then ran back to its owner. She had the reached the rollator, which had been torn away from her, and picked up the leash with the help of the handle of a cane that sat in a holder.

The Asian lady left her trolley and the chickens and made for the exit, gesturing to ward off the employees who held up their hands to stop her, telling her she couldn't just run off, but didn't actually hold her back when push came to shove.

Five minutes later we were outside Aldi, on a little square furnished with an artificial palm tree. Some sort of shop had put it there as part of their oasis theme. There was also a big cloth camel. Presumably it was supposed to be standing up, but it had toppled onto its side. Someone had burnt small round holes in its fur with a cigarette. I'd got the pensioner sitting on a bench, the dog in her lap and the rollator parked beside her. Waldemar sat in his wheelchair.

She was chatting. It had to be the shock. It was about chickens.

"I thought I'd have chicken tonight," she said, mechanically petting the dog. "With parsley and gravy and new potatoes."

Then she paused, stopped petting the dog, and said, "Cucumber salad." She didn't try and make a sentence out of it – it was just that one word, and she said it as if it were her last.

"Well, we can go back in and get a chicken," I said.

"The yellow woman took them," she said.

"No, um, she ran off."

"Yes, with the chickens. She took the chickens, there won't be any chicken tonight."

"She didn't take them. We just didn't buy any in all the confusion, but they're in there now."

"No, she took them."

"We're going in circles. Waldemar, shall I go inside and get two of the stupid chickens, if I can find two that haven't been pissed on?"

"That's not necessary," said Waldemar. He opened his parka, and inside, next to his stomach, were two rime-white chickens smoking with frost.

The pensioner looked at them like you'd look at a dead person suddenly brought to life before your eyes.

I understood from the conversation that the woman lived in the flat next to Waldemar's. It was the woman who had been observing me that first morning. She took one chicken and put it in the basket of the rollator. Then Waldemar and I looked at each other and began to laugh. It was the first time I saw Waldemar laugh. We waited expectantly for the man with wet trousers to come out of Aldi; we wanted to see him one more time. Then there was shouting and screaming further down the square. A crowd of boys came running up. They must have been about ten or eleven. Around their heads they had white ribbons of toilet paper, and two of them carried plastic Kalashnikovs, which they held in one hand and shot into the air. "Jihad, jihad, al-Qaeda jihad," they shouted as they rushed past. As they went, the one at the back snatched the chicken out of the rollator's basket and held it above his head like a trophy, howling, while they dashed on into MegaMetropolis and disappeared.

Waldemar took the consistent destructiveness in Stentofte with serene disregard; he'd become inured to it, and didn't move a muscle. I was astonished. The corners of the pensioner's mouth wobbled, but Waldemar said she could have his chicken, and put it in her basket. She adjusted it, as though to make sure it wasn't a mirage.

"Thank you," she said.

"Shall we go in and buy another chicken?" I asked.

"No," said Waldemar. "We'll go home. I've got some pasta."

Back at the apartment, Waldemar took the pegs out of their packaging and sat there turning them this way and that. He took out the Rawlplugs and the screws and put one of the screws into the hole in the peg to check it fitted.

"Are you good at this sort of thing?" he asked me.

"Not really. Do you have a drill?"

"A drill? Can't we use a screwdriver?" Waldemar went into the hallway, took a toolbox out of the cupboard and opened it. I peered over his shoulder into the box. Inside were a few cross-head screwdrivers.

"We can use these, but I don't think it'll be enough.

If we just screw the peg back into the old holes, it won't stay up. We need to drill new ones."

"So you're sure we need to use a drill?"

"Yeah, if you want it to stay up."

"Do you have one at home?"

"No."

"Hang on."

Waldemar took his phone out of his pocket and dialled.

"It's me," he said. "Do you have a drill? . . . Can I drop by and borrow it? . . . Fine, but we need it today."

I guessed he was talking to his parents. It didn't sound like they wanted him to come over, but they gave in. Waldemar said we would be there in less than an hour.

At least I'm getting a bit of a walk, I thought on the way to Waldemar's parents' place. They turned out to be archetypal Stentofte residents: in Stentofte, the most one could hope for were disability benefits. In Stentofte, the local council was an entity that occupied the bulk of one's existence, and the relationship one developed with it was the kind a teenager has with his parents. The local authority was simultaneously the great villain and the great provider. People maintained an image of the council as an enemy that had to be fought, regardless of the fact that the same authority was their only source of income. In Stentofte, they were experts on subsidies and public regulations. I thought I knew something about tax deductibles, but my knowledge was nothing compared to what the residents of Stentofte knew about subsidies.

Waldemar parked his wheelchair in the stairwell and we took the lift up to the fourth floor. The door was ajar. Waldemar's parents sat on the sofa in front of the TV. His mother was busy making a cigarette: she had a machine, a box of filters and a bag of tobacco in front of her, and she could roll cigarettes without taking her eyes off the screen.

"Have you complained?" she said as we entered the living room.

Apparently, Waldemar was supposed to complain about a caseworker who had obtained information from the pharmacy about his medical expenses without Waldemar's permission. They chatted back and forth, and it turned out Waldemar hadn't complained.

"They called from the local authority and apologised," he said.

"Make sure you get that bloody well sorted," said his mother, spitting yet another cigarette out of the machine. "They've got to know they can't take just take whatever liberties they please."

I thought I was going to be introduced, but they acted like I wasn't there. His father shut down the conversation by saying they were harsh, the people at the council. I think this was partly directed at me, although he didn't look in my direction. Just so I was clear who were the harsh ones. Then he said the drill was on the table in the hall.

Waldemar left with an admonishment to make sure

the local authority paid for the peg for my jacket, and then we were on our way.

As we stood in the hallway putting up the peg, we began to smell burning. We walked round the flat to see whether something was smouldering, but it wasn't until Waldemar opened the door that it became clear it was coming from outside. It reeked of burnt food.

"It's coming from the old lady's place," I said, and got down on my knees to peer through the letter slot. The fug that drifted out made me cough. I rang the doorbell and knocked, but nobody answered.

"I need to go in and sit down," said Waldemar.

"Okay, I'll go look in through the window."

The window to the hallway was ajar. Behind the glass, the flat was thick with smoke. Picking up a stick from the ground, I used it to lever up the hasp, then opened the window and clambered inside.

"Hello?" I yelled, but no one replied. The TV was thundering in the living room, but I went first into the kitchen, where the smoke seemed to be coming from. The oven was half open, the grill turned up to maximum, and beneath the glowing element was a chicken, burnt completely black, blistering and smoking. I switched off the oven and turned on the extractor fan. When I turned around, the dog that had tripped the fat man in Aldi was looking up at me. It followed me into the living room.

Something grey was poking over the back of an olive-green armchair in front of the television. I walked around to the other side. There she sat, her head tilted and her eyes shut. She's kicked the bucket, I thought at first, it looked so peaceful – but she was only sleeping. Her pupils moved beneath her eyelids. She was dreaming. I stood next to the little dog in the chicken smoke and watched her, uncertain what I should do. I was afraid she'd be scared if I woke her.

The TV remote was on the arm of the chair, and I picked it up and turned down the volume. As the noise quieted, she opened her eyes.

"Holger," she said, "I had such a lovely dream."

"I'm not Holger."

In an attempt to seem as unthreatening as possible, I sat down in a chair.

"I came over from your neighbour's place. Your chicken got burnt."

"The chicken!"

She got out of her chair.

"Bit smoky in here."

We went into the kitchen. She didn't need to bend very far down to see the blackened chicken in the oven.

"It's only fit for the bin. I can't understand it."

She fetched two potholders and pulled out the grill with the chicken on it, setting it on the hob.

"I wanted to give it a blast on the grill to make the skin crispy, but it didn't like that."

I said goodbye and let myself out. Waldemar was in the living room, resting. He wasn't feeling well after walking round the flat looking for the source of the smoke. When I told him about the lady, sitting there asleep in the chicken smoke, his shoulders jumped up and down and he laughed hoarsely at the floor, having to round his back even more to get enough air.

Waldemar asked if I wanted to eat with him before I went home. There wasn't much to go home to, so I said yes, please.

"I've got some pasta sauce in the freezer," he said. "Could you chuck it in the microwave and thaw it out? I need to sit here a while longer."

There were several bags in the freezer. They all contained something brown. I took one of them and went to show it to Waldemar.

"Is it this one?"

"Yep," he said.

I boiled the water for the pasta as I put the sauce in the microwave.

"Hey, Waldemar," I said.

"Yes," he said, from the living room.

"I was thinking. The lady next door, her dinner's been cremated."

"Cremated?"

"I mean, she's burnt it. Cremation is when you burn a body. I've just got a habit of using weird words."

"Right, okay."

"But I was thinking we could ask her if she wants to join us."

Waldemar didn't answer. At first I thought I'd crossed the line. I don't know why I felt so bad about her sitting in there all alone – she managed just fine every other night, after all. Maybe it was the absurdity of being hired to help a person who didn't need me, while she was wandering around next door and could definitely do with some help. Then he appeared in the doorway.

"Sure we can," he said.

We laid the table for three and went round to invite her. The bell had to be pressed for five minutes before something finally happened. Her name turned out to be Martha, and although we introduced ourselves she still seemed to think I was someone called Holger, following us into Waldemar's without question. I pulled out a chair for her and she sat down. *How lovely*, she kept saying.

The spaghetti was a struggle for her. Waldemar advised. "You need to twirl it around the fork, like this."

She looked at Waldemar and smiled.

"Yes, they're unruly little things."

She tried to turn the fork as Waldemar had demonstrated, but it didn't really work. Occasionally she had to help herself out a little with her fingers.

I was called Holger another few times, and every time I said I wasn't Holger, and every time it knocked us back to the beginning.

Then we ate in silence. Cutlery clinked against plates. At intervals someone cleared their throat. The odd strange sucking noise came from Martha. I thought at first it was when she sucked up the spaghetti, but it was evidently the sound she made when she sucked her dentures to the roof of her mouth.

We ignored her so she could work in peace. But after a few minutes there was a rattling in her throat, and when I looked up she was sitting with her head leant backwards and her eyes wide open, swallowing.

"Martha?" I said, ". . . Martha?"

"She can't breathe," said Waldemar as I jumped to my feet.

I tried clapping her on the back and grabbing her waist and squeezing, but she kept gasping in vain for air. I didn't dare squeeze too much – she seemed so fragile and light. Her mouth was open, and I looked in and saw something, stuck three fingers inside and grabbed a rope of stuck-together spaghetti, pulling it out of her throat. She gulped down air in one long pull, while I held up the rope between my fingers to show Waldemar. His expression switched from concern to a boyish smile, and he gave me a thumbs up.

Not long afterwards I walked back through Stentofte to the station, withstood the mute threats of random violence as I waited on the platform, and endured the train ride back in the growing dark. The windows in the carriage transformed into mirrors. We sank away from the light as though in a diving bell.

When I got home I could smell how badly the flat stank, and I saw how dirty it was. Clutter was everywhere, but my day at work had given me new energy – that's one of the paradoxes of work – and I had picked up the pace, a little bit, at least, so I cleaned up in the living room and took the rubbish down before showering and going to bed and sleeping the working man's good and solid sleep.

Absolutely there was a certain euphoria. Merely getting out of the flat and being distracted had helped, and I had no problems getting out of bed the next morning. I squeezed a fat dollop of Colgate onto my brush and brushed with vehement enthusiasm.

The thought that it was only temporary made the whole thing easier too. And as I said, there was something about Waldemar. I liked the way he'd snuck the chickens underneath his jacket in Aldi. Or I'm not sure exactly what I liked, but there was something. I thought of him standing his ground in that flat in Stentofte. He was a man under siege. Surrounded by idiots, attacked by disease. He was solitary; he was the most solitary person I had ever met. And that was another paradox, because he'd been closely watched his entire life. Ever since he was born, his family had had carers. When he was little, he'd slept with various machines pumping and sucking, keeping him alive in various ways, and there were people employed to look after those machines as he slept, and now that, because of his enormous stubbornness and despite the doctors' warnings, he simply refused to use those machines as he slept, he still had people employed to come every day. Thirty-seven hours a week he had me going down there, and he didn't question it. That was how life was for him: he had no friends; he had a carer. It was a mystery to me how such a thing was possible, but I found out later that Waldemar was much sicker on paper than he was in reality. Or rather, what I mean is that he was at least as sick in reality as he was on paper – he was as sick as anyone could possibly be, so sick that we healthy people can't even begin to understand it – but because of the aforementioned almost superhuman toughness he could do more than you'd think was feasible with all his ailments, and that was partly why I was so superfluous as a carer much of the time. That's why I said, wrongly, that he was less sick in reality than on paper. But Waldemar was used to carers. I don't think he considered the possibility that things might be different. What would he do with all that time alone? I was paid by the local authority, so my hours could not be cut. It would be a stupid strategy to give the authorities anything back.

Waldemar was eating Coco Pops with milk in front of the TV when my second day at work began. It turned out we both had a weakness for American reality television. They were showing a programme about a family that was struggling to make ends meet. A man with a giant chin gave them a new house, and now the family was wandering around with Chin Man and the mum at the front, and every time they went into a new room the mum would put her hands up to her face and say, *Oh my God*. "Oh my God," she said when a new door opened onto yet another newly furnished room. "Oh-my-God, ooooh my Gooooood." It sounded like the soundtrack to a porn film.

Wow, not bad, I might say, and Waldemar might put down the spoon into the brown milk and say, for example, *Yes, that's what's so unfair, that the prizes are so big in the USA*.

"Would you rather live in the USA?"

"Yeah, with those prizes!"

Now and again I took issue with this, and we might debate back and forth. At first I saw the statement as the result of under-stimulation, of stupidity, but it was also the result of Waldemar's great hope that there would be a miracle, that his life would suddenly change. It wasn't something we talked about, but it was reflected in our choice of programming. Another one we enjoyed watching had a title that, in light of all the wretchedness in Waldemar's existence, was tragic. It was called *Extreme Makeover*, and it consisted of a team of plastic surgeons, beauty experts and stylists taking a person and transforming them completely.

The unspoken hope of change, of something different and better, maybe even of health, bothered me. Not that there was something wrong with hoping, but it was in dismal contrast to our everyday lives, which were steeped in stagnation and external hopelessness.

Personally, I liked watching shows about fat people who had to lose weight, but that didn't strike a chord with Waldemar. He saw their excess weight as a minor inconvenience – what were fifty kilos of fat compared with Waldemar's ailments? Compared with Waldemar's ailments, the fat people's fat was a gift from heaven.

Waldemar didn't drink much – his body couldn't tolerate it – but he smoked the occasional joint. One of his ailments caused him pain that during certain periods could be quite strong, and apparently it helped to smoke hash. He offered some to me too, but I don't like smoking: first I get paranoid about everything and everybody, and then I get slow-witted. But Waldemar had a bottle of rum, and when he smoked I usually had a rum and Coke. That was Waldemar's preferred drink, and I agreed.

I think he smoked about once or twice a week. On average, because sometimes several weeks would pass without him smoking and other times he'd smoke four days in a row. It depended on the pain and what he felt like, he said. When he smoked we sat on the sofas, me with my rum and Coke and Waldemar with his carelessly rolled joint, and for long periods you could hear nothing but him inhaling and occasionally coughing quietly, and then the faint clinking of the ice cubes in my drink. Waldemar always had ice cubes in the freezer, and a small sandwich bag of hash in the top drawer of the chest of drawers. If he was running out we'd go down to where they sold hash and buy four grams, and that would last a while, because he wasn't a big smoker. It's important for me not to give that impression of Waldemar. He only smoked a bit. Other times we talked while we smoked and drank.

"We're going to the backgammon club today," said Waldemar, when there was only a small drop of brown milk and a single blanched Coco Pop left in the bowl.

The backgammon club was the place where they sold hash, a basement room a couple of blocks away. Waldemar parked his wheelchair by a skylight and together we went down the five steps and opened the mirrored-glass door. The basement room was lit by fluorescent tubes; there was a bar and a fridge and a sofa set around a low glass table. In the corner the TV was on, and a handful of people sat on the sofas, watching a sports programme. The place smelled of hash, and of the tobacco one of them was roasting by the glass table.

"Long time, Waldemar," said a guy behind the bar, putting his hand up for a high five. Waldemar smacked it. He struggled to reach, standing on his toes. Afterwards he gasped for breath.

"You got a new servant?" he asked, nodding towards me.

"This is my new carer."

"Hi, my name's Asger," I said.

The guy behind the bar was called Ahmed.

One of the men on the sofa asked Waldemar if he wanted to play some PlayStation, and Waldemar let himself be talked into a game and a joint. I bought a Coke and sat waiting at the bar.

A man about twenty years old came through the door. His name was Yusif, and instantly he started bickering with Ahmed in Arabic. After a while Yusif turned to me and explained that hash was haram.

"We know, Yusif, we don't care," said Ahmed. But Yusif waved him away and sat down to drink a Coke. He was Ahmed's brother, and turned out to be chatty. Not long ago, he started telling me, he'd got religious.

It was tough, being a new Muslim, he said. He was never sure what was halal. Was the nutmeg his mum used haram, for instance? Yusif gazed at me enquiringly. And of course he knew it was haram for a man to wear gold and silk, but what about the silver ring on his right ring finger – was a silver ring on a finger haram? He said he'd written to a fatwa service in Egypt and been told nutmeg in small quantities was halal, but it was haram for a man to wear silver. It was halal, however, to wear a silver ring that doubled as a stamp, but only if you needed to stamp things, and Allah knew best and peace be to Allah's messenger; Yusif didn't need to stamp things, and his ring couldn't stamp anything anyway, so it had ended up in the chest of drawers with the silk shirt, while his mum was still grating nutmeg in the kitchen with the fine side of the grater.

Did I know what nutmeg was?

"Oh yeah," I said. "It's like a nut."

Yusif kept talking. He'd let his beard grow. He'd started praying five times a day. The prophet Muhammad, may Allah's peace and blessings be upon him, said *prayer is the key to Paradise*, and he said *perform regular prayers, because prayer keeps people from shameful conduct*, and Yusif prayed between daybreak and sunrise, he prayed during midday, he prayed in the afternoon, and he prayed after sunset, and at night he prayed one last time, and it cleansed the soul; he never felt so good as on those mornings when he was the first person in the flat to wake and said his prayers while the morning light trickled in, for prayer was better than sleep.

Yusif had stopped masturbating, "I swear I've

stopped," he said, and his brother, who was listening behind the bar, laughed.

During a personal conversation, Stentofte's learned imam, Sharif, had emphasised to Yusif that masturbation was haram in itself, according to all recognised schools of law. But it was a confusing subject, admitted Yusif, because although masturbation was haram in itself, under certain circumstances it was permitted. If you masturbated because you were afraid of zina, then it wasn't haram, but only, said Yusif, stressing the word only, if you weren't able to get married. And since Yusif was of age and could marry, masturbation wasn't an option. The imam had talked about the pressure a young Muslim was under in an age where the senses were bombarded with porn, where there was nudity and sex in the media, and he'd advised Yusif to lower his gaze when he walked down the street, to look to the Koran when he felt weak, to read no other books or magazines, to not watch TV or go online. Allah would reward him with a beautiful woman he could marry. But the most important thing was still prayer. If Yusif prayed, the imam knew that he could endure, and Yusif prayed with zeal, and the praying helped.

Ahmed was rummaging restlessly behind the bar, and told Yusif to leave me alone.

"He's out of it," he apologised.

But his brother winked at me and insisted on giving me his phone number, saying he could put me in touch with Imam Sharif if I wanted to hear more. He was much better at talking about it.

Then Waldemar finished playing, and we left with stocks replenished.

That afternoon my second day of work was over. And the third came the next morning, and already they'd begun to intermingle.

When you walked among the housing blocks in Stentofte, you always found things destroyed. Umbrellas torn to shreds, smashed electronics, crushed or burnt toys. The children you met were often busy destroying something: breaking a newly planted birch tree in half or hurling an old radio against a wall.

Another telltale sign were the fires. Never a month went by without something being set on fire, be it a container or a car or, worst-case scenario, a building. The building that housed the after-school club had long since burned down and now stood empty; the town hall had also been set on fire a couple of times, but the attempts had either been amateurish or symbolic, because the fire had swiftly been put out.

When I think back to Stentofte, it was like everything anybody did was motivated by hatred and hopelessness. As though hatred oozed out of the concrete and slowly permeated the body, as though it was delivered in window envelopes from the council, lingering in the cat piss-infested sand in the sandpits and passed down to the younger generations like the family jewels. If hatred were a bacterium, Stentofte was a Petri dish, and if hatred were something that lived in us like a shoot, something we spent our lives holding down, then the air itself in Stentofte was fertiliser imbibed. People clumped together in fear and cultivated their contempt. I sensed it myself. And in talking about Stentofte there's no way around the racism and the deep mistrust that went both ways and made life even more unbearable for all the people in the blocks. As Waldemar said once, as we were passing a group of youngsters chattering in Arabic, it annoyed him they had a language we didn't understand when they could understand ours. It meant they could talk about us. The statement, like so many of Waldemar's statements, was as true as it was stupid, and I didn't know what to say. Otherwise it wasn't a problem that preoccupied Waldemar very much. His loathing of Stentofte ran deeper. But that Stentofte had been overrun by immigrants and that this had made things much worse was a perspective that emerged on the rare occasions when we spent time with his parents. Like the nice person I was, I kept silent when the conversation turned to immigrants, but it didn't take more than a month in Stentofte before irritation and contempt began to set in. When Waldemar's wheelchair was smashed up, my first thought was, *It's the immigrants.* I never said it aloud, but if you'd given me ten years in Stentofte, I would have.

The destruction of the wheelchair was the culmination of a series of smaller actions that started in the MegaMetropolis Aldi, where there was an offer on roast beef.

"Don't pensioners love that sort of thing?" said Waldemar.

"No, pensioners prefer something softer. They don't eat red meat."

"You don't think so."

"Um, no."

"Stop it."

"Stop what."

"Stop being a smartarse."

"Okay."

"So what do you think?"

"I think a pensioner could eat roast beef . . . Pensioners love roast beef."

"What about carers?"

"They're also crazy about roast beef. And gravy and new potatoes."

"Then that's what they shall have."

Waldemar threw some roast beef into the trolley I was pushing.

"Are you having a pensioner over for dinner?"

"I was thinking of asking Martha if she wanted to join us again. I could cut the meat into small pieces."

"It's a good idea to invite her."

"But I was thinking."

"Yes."

"Couldn't you just pretend to be Holger this time?"

I promised to pretend I was Holger. I didn't like play-acting, but Waldemar was right.

Waldemar had an electric meat thermometer, and we read up online about what temperature and setting the oven should be. When we stuck the needle of the thermometer into the roast beef before it went in, it reminded me for some reason of a small patient. I think it was because the kitchen was so clean, and the meat thermometer's digital display was white.

I was going to remark on this to Waldemar, but it would have been too strange, so I'm putting it here instead. I feel like it might be interesting to share that sort of observation and comment with one another. Like later on, when we opened the oven door and for a few seconds I fell into a reverie over the clouds at the bottom of the roasting pan. It was a whole world. There was a porous, coral-like reef of some brown, spongy thing in a lava lamp of tumbling fat and water. But where do we draw the line around what we can share? Stentofte we can share if we look at it from a distance, and Waldemar, if we observe him over a span of time. But the shorter the span, the harder the task. The skin on his face with its big pores, or a special look in his eyes as he peered through the glass oven door at what I now quite perversely thought of as the little patient – that might be more difficult, and the alien impression the tiniest things can convey in a short sudden second may be something we can't really share. Like the way Stentofte opened up after dark. You'd think it would have the opposite effect, that the lid would come down. But it wasn't like that. Things that would have been impossible to notice under a blue sky – perhaps a carpet hanging over a balcony three floors up – would attract your attention once the street lamps were lit. You looked up more. I wonder, possibly with a slight drumroll: is it the great darkness that draws the gaze upwards?

We went over to invite Martha. She didn't answer, not even after we'd rung for five minutes. I had to peep through the letterbox again. There was silence inside.

"Martha," I yelled, resting on my knees.

"She never goes out in the evening, so she should be in."

"Let's check the window."

The window was ajar, like last time.

"She should be more careful," said Waldemar as I lifted up the hasp. I think it was the same branch I used last time, still lying there.

"Do you think we could get in trouble?"

"Definitely," I said. "But she isn't aware of much, so why don't we take a chance instead of getting everybody else involved?"

"Yeah . . . I'm just going to head inside and rest on the stairs."

I climbed in through the window. The dog came puffing over and started sniffing my leg.

Martha was in bed. I shouted her name, but she didn't answer. When I got closer I could see her chin had dropped. I touched her arm, which was lying over the duvet. It was cold. I went out and opened the front door.

"She's dead," I told Waldemar, who was sitting on the stairs.

The dog squeaked in the kitchen. It had settled in front of the empty food bowl. I filled its water bowl from the tap and went through the cupboards to find a sachet of dog food. It started eating as I poured.

Waldemar stood in the bedroom doorway, looking at her.

"We'd better call someone," I said.

They fetched Martha in an ambulance without sirens. I said Waldemar had had a key to the flat. As they carried the body away, the dog began to howl.

"How do you comfort a dog?" said Waldemar.

"No idea."

Shortly afterwards a man came round, put it in a cage and then drove off with it.

When it was over we closed the door to Martha's flat and went back into ours to eat the roast beef.

"It's perfect," said Waldemar as he carved up. Martha's place was still laid: a plate with a knife and fork either side – and a wine glass, because he'd also bought a bottle of wine.

"Have you ever seen a dead person before?" I asked.

"Only on TV."

"To Martha," I said, raising my glass.

"To Martha," said Waldemar.

"What do you think will happen to the dog?" he said.

"Might end up at some sort of dog's home, I guess?"

"You don't think they'll just put it down?"

"I'm sure someone will want it. But I don't bloody know. Would you like a dog?"

"Not a little one like that."

"A dog's a dog, isn't it?"

"Nah, I'd rather have a big one. Not that I'd have a dog anyway. What about you?"

"No dog for me either."

"I don't like the thought of her dying all alone."

"No, nor do I . . . She missed out on some lovely roast beef, Waldemar."

"Think I'm going to smoke a joint. You want a rum and Coke?"

"A small one for the road would be nice."

We sat down with our drink and joint and watched TV. Later I walked back through Stentofte in the dusk and rode the train home.

Three days later, Martha was buried. We took the bus to Stentofte Church. It was a modern building, what one might call characteristically Scandinavian architecture. When we went inside we thought at first there was no one there besides us and Martha, who lay in her coffin. There were no lights on, but the church was illuminated indirectly by several rows of windows concealed from the eye in the roof, as though we were inside a massive tiered lamp. The wind blew fiercely outside, dark clouds arising rapidly and unravelling rapidly once more. When they blew across the sun the light in the church faded, as though night had abruptly fallen. The constantly shifting light made it seem like somebody was playing with a dimmer switch.

We sat down in the middle of the church. Waldemar asked me whether it was the priest who'd been standing outside, and I said I thought it was the parish curate. Then we were quiet for a while. Just to say something, I whispered, *Peter Piper picked a peck of pickled parish priests.*

Waldemar bit his bottom lip.

Behind us there was a dry, rasping sound. We both turned. In the very back row sat the kind of man who manages to blend in completely with his surroundings. It was as if he were half transparent and had brought his own darkness to sit in. He was holding a handkerchief to his mouth, so it was impossible to tell whether he was crying or coughing. After I'd turned around a couple of times, pretending to study the church's design and architecture, I became more and more convinced that he was laughing. But he could hardly have heard the line about the pickled priests, and although it went down well with Waldemar – and nothing was too infantile for me – the joke wasn't exactly likely to give someone a fit of the giggles. On the other hand, I supposed, it wasn't all that unusual to start laughing for no reason when someone had died. Waldemar, too, kept turning round for another glimpse of the man, whose presence felt like a draught at the back of our necks.

We got a chance to see him better when he stuffed his handkerchief into his pocket, rose to his feet and walked down the central aisle. As he passed us, we were struck by the musty scent of damp. He drew a banner of darkness in his wake like smoke from a torch.

He stopped at the coffin, his side turned towards us. When a cloud passed overhead, he was silhouetted against a candle a few metres behind him, but when the cloud drifted on we could see an empty face and the folds in his black clothes. The light kept changing like that, alternating, over and over. He put his right hand on the coffin. At that moment the light dimmed and the chestnut glow of the trees vanished and everything seemed as colourless as him. As though he'd sucked the colour from the coffin.

"Shit," whispered Waldemar.

The man looked at us. Then he lowered his gaze again and took his hand off the coffin and glided back down the aisle to his seat in the back row. Again there was that dank smell. We held our breath.

Then the priest appeared.

The ceremony was brief. In the middle of the first hymn another guest arrived, sitting at the front and singing in a creaky voice. I contented myself with staring down at my hymnal and mumbling, but Waldemar sang loud and clear and pure until he ran out of air. Not a sound from the man in the back row.

The coffin was carried out into a hearse by six black-clad men who'd been hired for the occasion. The priest said Martha would be driven to Stentofte Churchyard, five minutes away, and those who wished to were welcome to come and witness the burial.

The hearse drove through the outer edges of Stentofte towards the churchyard. The man who'd walked through the church and touched the coffin had vanished the moment it was carried out, but the one who'd showed up during the first hymn did come, and we formed a procession.

He went first, and I could see his reflection in the rear window of the hearse, hovering above Martha's coffin like a double exposure. He was dressed in the type of hopelessly thrown-together assortment of clothes people only wear if they've run out of time, and the world and all its codes have grown unfamiliar. On his feet were a pair of polished black leather shoes with tassels, his trousers were a pair of synthetic sweatpants – blue with a red stripe down the side – and on his upper body he wore a bright new white shirt with a wide black tie. On top of that was a beige cardigan. He lost a button as we walked. I picked it up but didn't give it to him – it seemed too silly, somehow, but it burned in my clenched fist throughout. His head was bald and covered in liver spots. The collar of his shirt gaped. We walked with great slowness through the empty streets.

I wondered who had arranged it all. A smaller ceremony would have done the job. The lid of the coffin was shiny, devoid of flowers or wreaths. We should have brought something. Or maybe we shouldn't have come at all. "Shall we go home?" I asked Waldemar as we left the church, but Waldemar, with his usual instinct for consistency, had been determined to persevere. "We're here now," he said. That was his final and, in his mind, entirely reasonable argument, and I already knew better than to try and discuss it.

After the priest had thrown soil on the coffin with a very fancy little silver shovel, there was a moment's silence and we all stood staring into the hole in the ground. She was buried under a small birch tree as the clouds still rushed past the sun in their counting-sheep-like way, making the shadows flash, and the wind tugged at the branches of the trees and at the priest's black robe, painting it against his thin legs.

"I'd like to say a few words," said the man in the bizarre get-up, and began. "Today we bury Martha. It's windy and cold. She's in her coffin, and somehow she's finally been proved right – she can't hear anymore and can't answer back anymore. So it would be best to be silent. My experience tells me it's usually best to be silent. But nobody learns from their experiences, there has never been a person who has learned from their experiences, and so now I'm standing here talking. On the subject of speaking, there's something I'd like to say: in my early youth, with the help of a sound technician, I listened to my voice played back on a wax disc. I was able to hear myself, which, I may say, I regretted, because I never again took quite the same pleasure in speaking: the voice inside my skull was far more harmonious than the voice I heard coming out of the phonograph. But during the recording process my upper lip touched the horn, and the taste has lodged in my memory throughout the years that have passed. The technician's face has long since been erased, but the taste of the horn and the shiver I felt at the fatuous sound of my voice, which nature had been kind enough to veil from me, I doubt will vanish until my own dying day. I think of the taste of metal almost every time I speak. It tasted of blood."

He paused and looked into the grave, turned the cardigan's remaining button a few times and continued. "Sorry, I'm getting lost. I'm an old man and I'm only talking about myself, but we should listen to people who talk about themselves, because they're really talking about everybody. That's the realisation I've reached after a lifetime of talking about myself and listening to other people also talking about themselves in the breaks between all this talk about myself. I'm going to die, like Martha, lying in her grave, did, and like all of you will too. And when we talk, we talk about nothing other than death, even though the words may pretend they mean something else. So it doesn't matter whether we're talking about ourselves or about someone else, because ultimately, and this is my firm conviction, we're talking about death. And at least now Martha is free of one thing: those who are dead are no longer forced to eat one another up the way we living are, but only to be eaten themselves. That's all I wanted to say . . . Sleep well, Martha . . . And to the worms down there: go to work with an appetite, comrades."

We left Stentofte Churchyard. Instead of taking the bus – neither of us could bear to be shut into anything – we agreed to walk home. We always called it walking, although only I actually walked. We didn't follow the bus route because it went the long way round, walking instead directly through what, from a purely geometrical standpoint, was the centre of Stentofte.

Waldemar's wheelchair ran off a battery that occasionally needed to be charged. The night before the funeral, I'd asked Waldemar: "Do you want to charge up your wheelchair?"

"No need," he said.

"But you're going into town tomorrow."

"There's still enough battery."

"But you just have to plug it in, then you'll be on the safe side."

"I'll charge it tomorrow."

"If you can't be bothered, let me do it."

"I can be bothered, it's just not necessary."

His unwillingness to charge the wheelchair's battery upset me. I saw it as an expression of apathy or laziness, a diminished capacity to take the least initiative, grounded perhaps in a permanent state of depression. And of course I wasn't allowed to charge the battery for him, not now it had become an issue, because by doing so, by charging the battery, I would underscore his indolence, show how easy it was to do the thing he wouldn't do. It was no big deal, after all, even for someone under the yoke of illness, like Waldemar, to get up and plug something in. Or maybe it was? Maybe, in fact, it was impossible for a healthy person to comprehend the extent of Waldemar's exhaustion as he sat there on the sofa, refusing to let me plug in the wheelchair – me, the healthy one, mocking him by accomplishing in a trice what he could not.

But the upshot, regardless, was that as we were walking through Stentofte, the wheelchair began to give out. The wind was against us, and if it would die down for half an hour so Waldemar didn't have to drive into a headwind, I thought, then we might have enough juice to get home. But the wind didn't die down, and we drove more and more slowly.

At last the wheelchair was moving more slowly than I could walk, and I had to stop and wait when I got too far ahead. Waldemar was silent. Then it ground to a halt.

"What do we do now?"

"We wait."

"Wait?"

"Sometimes it can go a bit further if you give it a break."

We waited a minute, then Waldemar started again. The wheelchair drove off very slowly, but after ten metres it stopped again.

"Shall I push it?"

"Hang on."

We waited another few minutes, and Waldemar started again. This time the wheelchair only moved a few metres at a snail's pace before stopping.

A particularly powerful gust of wind blew some dirt into my eye before I could turn away.

"Pull your top eyelid over the bottom one."

"Yeah, thanks, that's a classic trick."

"Is it out?"

"Not sure – it stings like hell. Yeah, there it goes, I think."

"It won't budge."

"Then I'll just push you home."

"You can't."

"No?"

"There's something wrong with the wheelchair. I can't disengage the engine."

"So it can't be pushed at all?"

"Nope."

"Let me try."

I tried to push the wheelchair. It gave a sluggish whirring noise and could only be shifted slowly. I had to place my whole weight behind it, and gave up after a few metres.

"You're pushing against the engine. This is the switch that doesn't work."

Waldemar flipped a switch back and forth without effect. And so there we stood – in the middle of the most desolate and windswept part of Stentofte, with a dead wheelchair and a white sun nearing the horizon. A group of young men sitting on a bench on the other side of the grass had caught sight of us and stopped their conversation.

"I don't get what's so hard about charging the wheelchair."

Waldemar didn't take the bait; he just glowered into space.

"How long has that switch been broken?"

"Ages."

"What do we do now?"

"We'll walk the rest of the way."

Waldemar got to his feet.

"What about the chair?"

"We'll have to leave it."

"Do you think it's wise to leave it in the middle of Stentofte?"

"Definitely not, but I want to go home now."

We started walking down the path. On one side was a housing block and on the other was the plane of grass. The lads on the bench had started crossing the grass. I decided not to look over my shoulder. Waldemar paid them no heed.

"Woah, he's fucked up his wheelchair," I heard them shouting behind us. I couldn't help casting one last glance back. They were standing in a ring around the chair.

We turned the corner, abandoning the chair to the mercy of Stentofte. I think it was two kilometres back to Waldemar's block.

"I'm not going to say anything because I need to save my breath," said Waldemar.

"Okay."

For a while we managed alright. Waldemar breathed heavily and walked slowly like an old man. I shoved my hands in my pockets and fingered my phone. I didn't want to take it out of my pocket, but I tried to remember when I'd last charged it up. A couple of days ago. I remembered because I'd spent half an hour looking for the charger, until it turned out it had been in the socket the whole time. I discovered a shred of meat between two molars and tried in vain to suck it out. Must be the chicken from yesterday. Good thing there was some battery left. That way I could phone for help if Waldemar collapsed.

Frankly, I could carry him. If it came to that, I thought.

"Let me know if you need an arm to lean on."

Waldemar waved a dismissive hand. He'd gone into a kind of trance, walking and staring at the asphalt with a face like a marathon runner, shutting out the pain and simply putting one foot in front of the other again and again.

It took us forty-five minutes to get home. The buildings grew black and the windows sprang out like glowing yellow rectangles. The areas of grass became murky depths. The wind abated and the clouds hung like colossal whales, their bellies lit by the dead light radiating from a sunken Stentofte. I bit back my sarcasm, although I was pretty irritated over the whole battery thing, because I was afraid he would die on this walk, and I thought no one should die while being scolded.

The wheelchair was bothering me too. I didn't like the thought of it being left out in Stentofte all night long. That's one of my strongest instincts: collecting my things. It feels unpleasant to spread out. It's the sense of something being left behind, being neglected. I've never had a house, but if I did I'd take a walk in the garden every night to make sure nothing had been left out on the lawn, abandoned to the dew and the dark. And later, when I'd go to bed that evening, it would be the last thing I'd think about, there on the path in the darkness of Stentofte.

At the main door Waldemar dropped his keys and sat down. I picked them up and unlocked the door and fastened it so it wouldn't slam. Going inside, I opened the door to the flat and hurried back outside, crouching down and putting my arms under Waldemar's, helping him inside and onto the sofa. He weighed nothing.

"I just need to lie down," he said, shutting his eyes.

I sat down on the chair without really knowing what I should do. Waldemar was breathing heavily. One arm hung over the edge of the sofa.

"I'm going to get a rum and Coke," I said. As though I'd earned a pick-me-up after the walk.

When I was back in the chair, Waldemar opened his eyes and said, "I think it's been three years since I walked that far. I can't take it anymore."

"Are you in pain?"

"All my muscles hurt. And there's a pain in my heart, and I can't breathe properly, but it'll be okay . . . Stupid battery."

"Yeah, that battery is dumb."

I ate dinner at home in front of the TV. Håkon suddenly appeared onscreen, and my fork froze before my lips. They were building a mountain in Herning. It was going to be five hundred metres tall and be made of a kind of artificial granite and soil. A politician from Herning spoke first, followed by Håkon. He had evidently been attached to the project as a PR man, and looked enthusiastic, chatting about thinking big and taking risks. "We won't let ourselves be cowed by conformism or false modesty," he said. "Herning shall have its mountain."

They cut to a politician from Silkeborg being interviewed on top of Himmelbjerget mountain. He was against the mountain in Herning. Then there was the weather report.

Next morning I had a text from Waldemar. He'd been admitted to the central hospital and asked me to see about the wheelchair. The company responsible for servicing it couldn't pick it up until the weekend, and it couldn't be left out in Stentofte that long. The text didn't say what Waldemar had been admitted for, but previously he'd told me he was hospitalised now and then when his condition got so bad he had to stay under observation.

After picking up an extra battery at a wheelchair centre in Vanløse, I arrived in Stentofte with the battery in my shoulder bag. The wheelchair stood where we had left it. The padding had been torn open and everything loose had been ripped off. It was surrounded by glittering pieces of plastic from the smashed reflectors. But the destruction was half-hearted, absent-minded, because when I inserted the new battery, following the instructions of the man from the wheelchair centre, it started working again.

It was solid. The plastic ball on the joystick had come off, but I could still hold it and steer. The on-and-off button had been crushed and cut my fingers, but it still worked.

At first I tried walking next to the wheelchair while I steered it, but gave up by the time I reached the first corner, and sat down in the seat instead. Hopelessness turned out to be like smog – it got thicker the closer you got to the asphalt, and at wheelchair-height I could really slurp it up. Stentofte was empty this early in the morning. The air was gritty and flickering with cold. I rode back to Waldemar's and let myself in with the spare key he'd given me, and parked the wheelchair in the hall. I had a quick nose around the flat, struck once more by its sterility, and decided to visit Waldemar in hospital later that day.

I took the lift ten floors up and walked down a corridor that smelled of food. Waldemar was in bed, playing *Tekken* with the man he was sharing a room with, a giant in his late twenties whose face was open and happy and round. The PlayStation controller looked small as doll's furniture in his hands. He was twisting with excitement as he played, as though he had to pee.

"Shit," he kept yelling, "shit, shit, shit."

"You're getting your arse kicked," said Waldemar. He was lying very still with the controller, gazing in concentration at the screen, which hung on the wall above the beds, operating a little man with a grey beard, who suddenly finished the battle by standing on his hands and firing a series of kicks at his opponent's head. There were a few explosion-like smacks, and the opponent collapsed with a groan. His roommate relaxed and the bed stopped creaking. Then he picked up the remote and switched off the TV. "Shit," he said, one last time.

I knocked on the door frame where I'd been standing, watching.

"Hey," said Waldemar. "Herbert, we've got a visitor."

Herbert had stopped moving. He was lying with two pillows behind his head, staring into space as though philosophising over his defeat. Then, shaking himself out of whatever had been preoccupying him, he said hello. I waved and went to stand by the window. I gazed down at the city and the water. At the edge of my vision, Sweden was wedged in a bluish-grey vice of sky and sea.

"Hey, there's Sweden," I said.

"Still?" said Waldemar.

Herbert sat up in bed to check. Then he started telling us about an elk shawarma he'd once had in Malmö. He was about to have a few biopsies taken with a long needle and was clearly nervous, because he talked the entire time – mostly about his girlfriend, whom he'd met at a youth mental health centre. It sounded like a cute story, as far as I understood it, except that he kept turning it into something sleazy by saying stuff like when he got out of hospital he was going to get laid. His way of including Waldemar was to ask if he was going to go home and get laid too, to which Waldemar said no and started talking about something else. After a few minutes, a nurse and an orderly came by to fetch Herbert. The orderly had brought a wheelchair.

"I can walk, no problem," said Herbert, but the nurse said it was best to ride in the chair until they'd examined him and were sure they knew what was wrong. Herbert put on a hospital gown and sat in the wheelchair.

"Never done this before, riding around like this," he said, and as the orderly began to push he laughed like someone was tickling his belly. "Goodbye you two, I'm off for a check-up," and then he got that pensive, quiet look on his face again as they rolled him out the door.

Waldemar said he wanted to go outside. He stood up and put his parka over his pyjamas, stuck his feet in his shoes without lacing them and set off in the collapsible wheelchair beside his bed.

We took the lift down. I thought we'd be getting off at ground level, but we kept going down to the basement, and on Waldemar's instructions I pushed him down long corridors to a gate that opened onto a kind of loading and unloading dock below street level.

"This is a good place to smoke a joint."

"The doctors don't care?"

"I'm going home tomorrow, they're done examining me. They're just keeping me one more night to be sure I don't collapse again as soon as I get home."

"Were they able to tell you anything new?"

"Nothing except that I'm worse since last time, but I knew that already."

Two men loaded some empty pallets onto a truck. The light was dwindling. It was cold, and there was damp in the air. Waldemar seemed down. I couldn't think of anything to say, so we just stood there staring as he smoked.

"Want a puff?"

"Oh, go on then," I said, taking a puff from the wet end. I held the smoke in my lungs for a bit before puffing it back out into the damp air. It hung there like a cloud, drifting away from the gate and disintegrating. It worked almost instantly.

Waldemar sent a cloud after mine. Then he talked, still gazing into space. "I have no friends, I have no girlfriend and my family can't be arsed to spend time with me. I was only interesting to my parents when they could use me to get money from the council."

"You're exaggerating, Waldemar."

"I remember they used to call me the gold nugget, but only recently I realised it was . . ."

"Ironic?"

"Yeah."

"Do you think maybe the hospital is making you gloomy about things?"

"Not like it's much fun being in Stentofte either."

The men had finished loading up. They got into their truck and drove off.

"You know what?" I said. "We need to get out of Stentofte."

"Where should we go?"

"Well, I don't know. Just away."

"I can apply to the council, maybe."

"Yeah, apply to the council for something."

"Maybe we could go to Sweden?"

"Sure, but I was thinking even further away. Somewhere where it's warm."

"We went on a road trip to the Harz once, Mum and Dad and me. That was awesome."

"You can forget about the Harz."

"Nah, nah, it was more the road trip that was fun. Sitting there looking out the window . . . But I don't have a driving licence."

"But I do. All we need is to get hold of a car."

"Maybe the council can give us a grant."

"Jeez, shut up about the council for a minute."

"The council, the council, the council," he said stubbornly, taking a puff of his joint. I could see the thought had livened him up.

"There was a big gnome made of wood."

"Where?"

"Outside the hotel in the Harz."

"Okay, you need to stop going on about the Harz," I said.

"And mountains and fields with little purple flowers. Dad lifted me up so I could ride a cow with a bell around its neck."

"But hey, we can drive through the Alps if you want to go south, there's loads of that stuff. Then you can ride your cow there."

"I only want to go to the Harz."

"But . . ."

"No! Only the Harz."

"Calm down."

"Harz, Harz, Harz," he jeered like a child.

I looked down at him. He was gazing straight ahead, smiling.

"You're taking the piss."

He handed me the joint.

"We need to get out of Stentofte," I said, sending off another cloud. "We need to get the hell out of Stentofte, and it can't come soon enough."

But a few days later we were back in Stentofte. The weather was starting to get warmer, and that morning I'd even unbuttoned my jacket on my way through the concrete labyrinth. The birch trees that weren't snapped in half or burned had started putting out small green buds. Outside the kitchen window the grass was turning green, and all this sprouting did something to us, gave us itchy feet. Yet there was something unsaid between us as we sat on the sofa watching television, for neither of us had mentioned our travel plans since that evening at the hospital: we were usually a bit reserved around each other, but there we'd spoken more bluntly than usual, and now that we were back to our customary reserve, where the conversation rarely got all that candid, it was difficult to raise the matter again. It was like having made a far-too audacious plan while drunk.

On the television two women in leotards were standing opposite each other on a beam, fighting like Robin Hood and Little John in an attempt to throw the other onto a mattress a few metres under the beam. The staves they were armed with had either red or blue balls at both ends, and were too heavy for anything but half-hearted flapping and shoving. One of them sacrificed her balance to get in a decisive jab, but fell onto the mattress herself. The woman left on the beam assumed an ape-like victory pose.

"That's too lame," I said, changing the channel. This was a privilege I'd earned after a couple of weeks – the right to change the channel on an equal footing with Waldemar. We switched over in time to see Chin Man walk into a sparkling new house with a family who were crying for joy. "Oh my Gooood," we both said in chorus, at the same time as the housewife when Chin Man opened the kitchen door.

"Oh my Goooooood," Waldemar suddenly howled again, as though something had stabbed him. Then, leaping up as best he could, he ran to the toilet door and said, "Oh my Gooooood," and I got up and ran after him and peered over his shoulder while I shouted, "Oh my Gooood," and held my hands to my head, then I stampeded over to the fridge and opened it and screamed, "Oh my Gooood, Oh my Gooood, Oh my Gooood," staring into the white light. Waldemar came dashing after me and threw all the kitchen cupboards open one by one while we both went, "Oh my Gooood," in different tones of voice for every cupboard. I accompanied opening the cupboard with the plates with a kind of shrieking falsetto *oh my Gooood*, as though I were swooning over the contents, whereas when Waldemar opened the one with the Coco Pops and the bags of old flour it was more along the lines of a thunderstruck horror-movie whisper. When there were no more cupboards to open, calm descended. We stood there snorting among the gaping cupboards. I closed the fridge. Waldemar was pale with all the running and shouting.

"I have to go sit down," he wheezed.

"Can I bring you anything?"

"A glass of water, please. I'm seeing spots."

He'd reached the living room. I was still in the kitchen.

"You don't want a rum and Coke?"

"Would you like one?"

"Why not?"

"As the grill guy would say."

"Exactly."

As the grill guy would say gradually became a stock phrase for us. One of us would go, *Why not?* and then the other would go, *As the grill guy would say.* Sometimes we'd content ourselves with simply saying, *What would the grill guy say?* It came from Plato's Grill and Pizzeria, which was located in a small low building where the concrete slum ended. Once in a while we went down to pick up a pizza for lunch, and Waldemar always had a Viking with extra olives, and the man at the grill and pizzeria, the one we called the grill guy, always said, *Why not?* when Waldemar gave his order. I didn't order anything fancy; I just stuck to the menu, so I didn't get a *why not?* with mine.

"I'll pour you a pick-me-up, then," I said from the kitchen.

I'd brought a new bottle of rum round to Waldemar's. I was the one who'd drunk most of his old one anyway. Waldemar liked having things in stock. He had a huge selection of soft drinks in various colours in the fridge, but he very rarely drank any of them, and if one finally did get depleted then he made sure to buy another one the next day, even if he had three others like it already. I called it his battery. Whenever he put a soft drink in the basket, I'd say, *Do you need to charge the battery?* And Waldemar would reply something along the lines of, *Yeah, sure looks that way* or *You bet* or maybe simply *We need more soft drinks.* I think they amused him, these little variations on a theme. It amused him to be jovial.

The TV was still on, but a new programme had started. It was a food show.

"Oh," said Waldemar.

Moments later he was at his computer on the desk, switching it on. He sat there for a while, but when I walked past he closed the window.

"What are you doing there?" I asked.

"Just something."

One day, as we were watching TV, it was like a hand came out of the screen and grabbed me by the throat. It was a feature on Herning: they'd started building the mountain, and Håkon danced around in front of the camera, threw out his arms and said, "This is going to be big, we're pinching ourselves." The architect appeared too and explained what the mountain would mean for the residents of Herning and the surrounding areas, and an engineer, who was puffed up with nerves, described the materials and method of construction. But it couldn't all be fun and games, so they also featured a family whose house would end up in the shadow of the mountain. The man held a baby in his arms, standing with his wife and young daughter beside him, and said they'd have to sell – if anybody even wanted to buy.

That day I had to struggle home. I collapsed on the sofa. The mountain made me desperate and downcast to the very core of my heart. There was a sense of being utterly discarded. Håkon had a mountain; I had a disabled man in Stentofte. The job could still be called temporary. Yet I had the creeping feeling that it was my last stop, and not a springboard to something different and better. The hopelessness was so complete it restricted my breathing. And it didn't make me feel any better knowing that something as thoroughly silly as an artificial mountain had triggered it.

I was on the verge of calling Sara; I had the phone all the way out of my pocket. But I'd decided not to call anymore. Sitting there with the phone in my hand, I stuck to my decision. I don't know why. It was the last time I considered calling.

As I was falling asleep, it appeared, the mountain. It loomed above Herning at the centre of a massive storm. Lightning struck the peak, where Håkon stood with arms outstretched towards the sky, laughing diabolically. Horses ringed with flame galloped in circles around its foot.

The next day at work, Waldemar was back at the computer, acting all secretive, and again he wouldn't say what he was doing. Otherwise the days passed quietly with errands to MegaMetropolis and the backgammon club and the occasional trip into Copenhagen to buy some sort of electronic gadget.

One evening in Sydhavnen I was eating a frozen lasagne in front of my laptop while reading the news online. There was the usual crap, but one article in the tabloids did catch my attention: *Watch Out for Exploding Remoulade.* I clicked, and it turned out some containers of remoulade had exploded at the supermarket because it had fermented, and now they'd recalled the batch so that nobody needed to be afraid of being blasted with yellow sauce. To the right of the article were links to other food stories, and the headlines were:

Fake Pine Nuts Are Paralysing Your Taste Buds

Danes Getting Sick from Faeces Fruit

Supermarket Frozen Pizza Found to Contain Glass Shards

Selling Tinned Food as Homemade

Mouse Droppings Found in Rum Balls

The last one, *Mouse Droppings Found in Rum Balls*, I found especially hard to shake, and I was repeating it to myself all evening. It reminded me of the glowing freezer cabinets in Aldi, brewing their heavy mists of frost, and it was the last thing I intoned before I fell asleep: *Mouse Droppings Found in Rum Balls.* By now Waldemar was my only social contact, and after repeating the sentence on the train all the way to Stentofte, I said it to him, but it didn't really go down well.

After I'd done the cleaning I sat down at the computer and googled Yummy Dreams, the company who had produced the offending rum balls, and the mere fact that they were located in Lolland made me cry laughing, and when Waldemar saw me crying in front of the computer, going, *It's in Lolland, oh, no-no-no, dear God, it's in Lolland,* while I pointed at the screen through my tears, he too began to laugh. Suddenly he saw the genius of it. Or no, it wasn't genius, it was dumb-ius – something so dumb it swings back round and becomes great.

It became one of our stock phrases, *yummy dreams,* and it could mean anything. A particularly disgusting, filthy and urine-drenched toilet in a park in Stentofte, where the bushes had streamers of used toilet paper, could be *yummy dreams,* but so could the hotdogs he made one afternoon before we watched television, which also turned out to be pure *yummy dreams.* Waldemar instantly called a girl cycling along in a summer dress *yummy dreams*; but a homeless man hawking up a big green gobbet onto the asphalt could also prompt a *mmm, yummy dreams, straight from Lolland, they say*. At first he hadn't got it, but afterwards he turned out to be a big fan of the expression. To someone not in on the joke, of course, it sounded clunky in this really hair-brained way, but we loved saying *yummy dreams*, because the contrast between the hysterical name and the unsanitary rum balls summed up the idiocy we saw around us daily.

Another expression we enjoyed was *high pillows for side sleepers*. We picked it up on a trip to Ikea, when Waldemar wanted a new lamp. It was written on a completely dumb-ius diagram in the bedding department, where you could determine from your sleeping position – back, stomach, side, etc. – which size of pillow you needed. We said it constantly. It outcompeted *yummy dreams* for a while, and when we tired of simply saying *high pillows for side sleepers* and of asking in shops whether they had high pillows for side sleepers, we started doing small variations on the theme, and a conversation like this might play out:

"Do you need a new pillow soon, Waldemar?"

"Yup."

"How high should the pillow be?"

"It needs to be crazy high."

"Why?"

"Because I'm a side sleeper."

One day this culminated in us applying to the local authority for a higher pillow for Waldemar. Our reasoning was that we'd discovered he was a side sleeper. The caseworker wanted to see documentation from the doctor, and we got Waldemar's doctor to write an explanation saying that for health reasons Waldemar had to have a high pillow. And then we got our pillow-related carte blanche from the council and went to Ikea, and we'd agreed Waldemar should say, *My name is Waldemar, and I'm a side sleeper. I'd like the highest pillow you have.*

Outside Ikea we smoked a joint. As Waldemar rolled up to the sliding doors in his wheelchair with me by his side, and the glass slid aside with a hiss, I said, "You hear that, Waldemar? Those are the doors to pillow heaven, opening wide."

On our way to the department with the pillows and duvets and all that stuff, we went through the furniture department, and there was a particular chair that caught our attention, because it was called Bonkinnet, and I shouted, "Look, they've got a chair that's called Bonk-in-it," and we both sobbed with laughter, and I had to sit in the chair and recover for a minute. Then a married couple in their late thirties walked past, looking unspeakably self-important. They were clearly considering buying a Bonkinnet, so I got up to let them examine it in peace, and said, "It's a lovely chair," but they didn't dignify us with an answer. In the bathroom department I looked at my reflection in the mirror. My eyes were red with hash.

When we found a sales assistant to direct us to the bedding department, Waldemar didn't quite stick to the script, but that made it even better. He said, "Do you have high pillows?"

And the sales assistant, a man in his mid-twenties who for some reason was incredibly energetic, said, "We're really strong in pillows," and this answer completely winded Waldemar and me, and when we said nothing, and I had to turn away and bite my lip, the sales assistant said, "How high should it be?"

"Towering," said Waldemar. "I'm a side sleeper." Then his face started twitching weirdly and tears rolled down his cheeks, but the sales assistant ignored it, presumably thinking it was part of his disability, and he said, "Follow me," and as we walked he said, "There's also the question of firmness."

After buying the pillow we ate meatballs in the cafeteria, and Waldemar insisted his new pillow should lie on the table, and that the plate of meatballs should be on top of the pillow, and it was elevated so much he could barely reach, and only his eyes floated over the plate.

"That's a bloody high pillow," I said.

"It's a proper side-sleeping pillow."

"You'll break your neck if you turn over in your sleep."

"That's the way we side sleepers like it."

And we kept going like that.

The urge to repeat a mantra stemmed from the fact that we spent such enormous amounts of time doing nothing, or at least doing things that were a hair's breadth from doing nothing at all. From the fact that we had to fill out the time with excursions into town to buy superfluous things that no one alive actually needed, had to clean the flat even when it was already clean, had to go to the post office and pay rent on a home that wasn't a home, but an enemy of all life. And when the emptiness occasionally threatened to break through the thin veneer we were constantly painting over it with our silly chores, saying something even sillier helped to conjure the emptiness away. Sure, there was an element of *horror vacui* about it, like when workmen whistle or turn up the radio, but it was also a counter-attack, and nowhere did we see the evil and hypocrisy more clearly than in a sentence like *high pillows for side sleepers*; we saw the consistent perversion of everything, and then we could do nothing but laugh. After a while, as we developed this special form of self-preservation humour, a letter from the citizens' advisory service could make us hiccup with laughter when I read it aloud in the right tone of voice. Yes, in time it was as though you could tickle our feet simply by mentioning something like the citizens' advisory service. We'd long since stopped being citizens. Calling us that added insult to injury. We had to laugh.

Then one day it became apparent what Waldemar had been plotting on the computer. "Have you ever been to Morocco?" he opened by asking, and I said, "Erm, no."

"But have you heard of Torbi el Mekki from Skhirat?" said Waldemar.

"My old friend Torbi from Morocco," I said, "of course I've heard of Torbi," but Waldemar ignored my sarcasm and kept talking about Torbi el Mekki, who turned out to be a healer he'd found online. Waldemar said he healed people with serious illnesses, that people had thrown away their crutches after a visit, that they'd been able to see again, they'd been able to walk.

"But that's all bollocks, Waldemar."

"You can google him yourself, he's real enough."

"I don't doubt he's real. It's this guff about being able to cure anything and everything that I don't believe."

"Okay, well, I believe it . . . Anyway, he does it for free. If he were a conman, he'd take money for it."

"You don't think it seems kind of bonkers that some man in Morocco can just heal illnesses with his bare hands?"

"No."

"I don't know what to say . . . I didn't think you were that stupid."

Waldemar got up from the sofa, went into the bedroom and shut the door.

I stayed seated and switched on the TV, annoyed at myself and annoyed at the stupidity. *Extreme Makeover* was on. After ten minutes Waldemar still hadn't come out. I got up and went to knock on the door.

"This friend of yours in Morocco," I said. "If nothing else it could be a fun trip down."

"I'm getting a driving licence and driving down there by myself," he answered through the closed door.

"Yeah, but I'd like to come too. We can take a ferry from Gibraltar."

There was a short silence inside.

"Gibraltar, that sounds crazy."

I made coffee, and we sat down at the coffee table to form a plan.

"The first thing we've got to do is apply to the council," said Waldemar.

"What should we apply for?"

"A salary for you, among other things, and a grant for a car. There are loads of things."

"Do you have any money saved up?"

"I've got ten thousand."

"I'll still get my salary even if we leave, and I can borrow money from one of my friends, so I have a bit extra. If we drop the council stuff, we can set off next week."

"It's stupid to pass up free money if we can get it."

"It'll take forever."

"Three weeks," said Waldemar, holding up three fingers in the air. "Three weeks, tops. Plus we need to get a car."

For the time being I gave up trying to understand Waldemar's sudden fixation on an idea that seemed, if not exactly pulled out of thin air – he'd clearly been researching it online – then at least a tad random. And although I felt a powerful sense of animosity bordering on hatred towards this healer in Morocco and what he stood for, I was also eager to get away. I was desperate for any initiative whatsoever that would break the swing of the pendulum between the two poles of hopelessness: my flat in Sydhavnen and my workplace in Stentofte. And then it struck me that this was, in fact, the part of Waldemar's plan I fully understood: it was about getting away. Far away.

Waldemar began his negotiations with the caseworker. After a few days he was called in for a meeting. "It's best if you come too," he told me. The citizens' advisory service was in a building not far from Stentofte Town Hall.

I won't forget the caseworker until the day I die. A long black hair was growing out of a mole on his neck. But first may I say that nobody could wait like Waldemar: he sat in his wheelchair with the dignity of a samurai, watching the numbers on the board, which ticked up with mocking slowness towards the number he'd received by pressing the button on the machine by the entrance. And when we were finally sitting in front of the caseworker, and the pig began to pull out his nose hairs by gripping right beneath one nostril with the finger and thumb of his right hand and jerking his head backwards, before inspecting the catch then casting it into the wastepaper basket, not a muscle of Waldemar's face moved. He simply laid out a convincing case. He'd even made a little budget in

Excel, which included expenses like petrol, overnight costs and food.

I caught words and sentences like *additional expenditures due to disability* and *medical opinion*, and *beneficial effect of the heat*. Waldemar's doctor had written a statement saying that a trip would do Waldemar good. In every sense. Yes, it had been scientifically proven that the heat would help several of his ailments, and the caseworker attached great importance to that. That it had been proven. Scientifically. Fundamentally, however, I found the conversation incomprehensible, because of the nose-hair extraction. His nostril became an open drain; all thought, all words swirled around it like a whirlpool. Waldemar was entitled to additional expenses according to regulation §100. The caseworker let a nose hair drift down. Waldemar had put forward a sensible budget. The caseworker gave another tug, but this time had nothing to show for it.

Then, at last, the session seemed to be over. The caseworker said he was sure it would work out, he definitely thought so: Waldemar was going to Morocco. He held out his hand to Waldemar and Waldemar took it, and he wished Waldemar well and said they'd speak soon. But when he was about to say goodbye to me, he first put his fingers up to his nose to find a hair to tug at, changed his mind after letting them tap briefly against his upper lip, then offered me his hand, smiling. My own was already half outstretched, but dislike of his person took over, and instead of a handshake I grabbed the hair growing out of his mole with two fingers, plucked it out, held it in front of his eyes, then let it descend.

His face twisted briefly in pain and surprise, then went utterly dead and cold. He looked me directly in the eye for a beat, then went to open the door and said, "Goodbye, both of you. You can bet you'll be hearing from me."

Waldemar rolled out the door after me, and it was slammed behind us.

"Argh, for Christ's sake. Argh, for Christ's sake, jeez," he said.

I apologised the whole way back to the flat, but when Waldemar remained angry, I tried an attack.

"You couldn't have warned me we were meeting a freak? And why did I even have to come?"

"It was so he could see I needed a carer the whole time, but it was a bad idea."

A few days later the letter arrived. It said Waldemar had been rejected.

But Waldemar was undaunted, and insisted on resuming negotiations with his caseworker. A week had passed since the episode, and then he said he was meeting him the next day. And that I should come along to say sorry.

"You don't mean that," I said.

"If you want to go to Morocco, you've got to say sorry. It's the only way we're getting that money. I know this guy – he needs an apology."

The caseworker was beaming when we arrived. He was rubbing his hands and smirking and treating us with the friendliness of someone who knows they've got the upper hand. We took our seats in front of the desk and he took his behind it. Staring fixedly at me, he plucked out a nose hair, let it drift down into the wastepaper basket with the air of Mussolini, and said, "Well?"

Waldemar looked at me.

"Right. I wanted to say sorry for what happened last time."

The caseworker shut his eyes a moment. I looked enquiringly at Waldemar, but there was no help from that corner. When the caseworker said nothing, I assumed he wasn't satisfied with the apology yet, so I continued.

"It was thoroughly inappropriate pulling the hair out. It was a really bad joke."

"It wasn't a joke, it was outright assault."

"Oh, I mean, let's not . . ."

"It was assault. You assaulted me in my own office."

"You're right, I apologise . . . All I can do is apologise."

There was silence for a while.

"Am I to understand, then, that you're willing to reconsider the case? It would be a shame if Waldemar had to suffer for my stupidity."

More silence, so I added, "My completely absurd stupidity."

The caseworker smoothed one eyebrow with spit. Then he picked up a white plastic cup from the table and held it up between two fingers.

"You see this plastic cup?"

We both assumed it was a rhetorical question, but when nobody answered he said again, "Do you *see* this *cup*?"

"Yes," we said.

"Good," he replied. Then he got up, walked across the room, lifted down a fern from a square table in the corner of the office and put it on the floor, then moved the table so it was about a metre from the window. Then he opened the window and put the plastic cup upside down on the table.

"Now see here," he said. Sitting back in his chair, he opened a drawer and took out a ruler that was nearly as long as the drawer itself, then placed it on the table.

"If Waldemar can knock the cup out of the window with this ruler, then maybe we can sort things out . . . If he can't, then nobody's going to Morocco. He's got one try." Then he laughed, baring his teeth. A high, shrill laugh. For the rest of my life he will represent for me a symbol of all the world's evil; I can't imagine anything that would top him.

There was no point discussing it any further. Waldemar took the ruler and positioned himself by the square table. I've never seen a movement more awkward than when he hit that cup. It reminded me of myself during secondary-school PE. The cup landed on the floor.

"That's a shame," said the caseworker.

We left the office.

I mixed two rum and Cokes. Waldemar rolled a joint, speaking in disjoined sentences.

"I thought I had a chance . . . The cup weighed nothing."

"There was nothing we could do," I said. The ice cubes clinked mournfully. Waldemar lit the joint. "We'd already lost. You can't do anything against a petty little Hitler like that. You've always already bloody lost."

We sat staring into space. Waldemar handed me the joint.

"Let's listen to some music," I said, going over to the stereo. Waldemar had an excellent sound system he plugged into the TV when he wanted to play PlayStation, but he didn't really have any music. I'd brought my MacBook to work and connected it to the amplifier. I played the Misfits' first album, *Static Age*. We sat listening to a few tracks in silence. Waldemar sang along softly to "Last Caress":

Sweet lovely death
I am waiting for your breath
Come sweet death, one last caress.

He'd gone nuts for the Misfits after I'd introduced him to them.

"The whole thing's one big humiliation. I'll die before I ever get out of Stentofte."

"You mustn't say that."

"Crap," was all he said, staring into space.

Now, however, things began to pick up steam. When I got home that night, I said to myself, *Hang on a minute, over my dead bloody body!* and rang a friend who worked at a free newspaper. He sounded sceptical, but must have passed the story on because the next day I had a call from a tabloid journalist, who wanted to hear more. And later that week we were in the paper – with a picture of Waldemar in his wheelchair, and statements from me and Waldemar and the caseworker's boss. But it didn't stop there. Waldemar went on morning TV to tell his story. About the healer in Morocco who was his last hope, about the caseworker's psychological terrorism. He got a haircut at a barber's in Stentofte, and we considered a new pair of glasses too, but agreed that the old ones were best suited to the job – he couldn't look too expensive. I stayed backstage, eating a few fancy sandwiches, drinking five cups of sour coffee and giving Waldemar pep talks while the make-up lady battled with his skin. I was nervous – bricking it, in fact

– but Waldemar had smoked a fat joint that morning and it was helping his nerves. When they told us it was time and Waldemar went to sit on the sofa I was seized by panic, picturing how awkward it would surely be, but no. He coped with aplomb. There wasn't a dry eye in front of the TV, I'm sure, and I thought, *With a bit of luck there'll be a public outcry, people demanding Waldemar go to Morocco.*

A man by the name of Jacob Fitzer turned out to be watching TV that morning. A veteran of the '68 student riots, he'd got stinking rich selling a health food product on the shopping channel – a product that must have had at least a few human lives on its conscience. Now he was enjoying his retirement on a private island somewhere in the South Funen Archipelago. Whether he did it for the free advertising, whether it was part of a burning enthusiasm for alternative therapies or whether it was altruism pure and simple, we never discovered, but at any rate he decided to sponsor Waldemar's journey to the tune of seventy thousand kroner, handing it over with a giant cheque bearing the health food company's logo. It was called – no lie – Power-Trition, a portmanteau of *power* and *nutrition*, which he told me after the presentation of the cheque because I stupidly mentioned that I'd worked in the advertising business. He thought I might be interested in this little pearl of linguistic invention, which he'd come up with some time in the mid-eighties to sell bone meal with apparently marvellous properties to American housewives with severe anxiety. There was a photographer present when Waldemar was given the cheque at the Power-Trition HQ in Copenhagen, and they certainly talked a big game, but I'm not sure anything else happened in the media. Yeah, we were featured in some happy handicapped story in the TV guide, but apart from that people were already sick of Waldemar's diseases, and we couldn't have cared less, because now we had a massive cheque for seventy-thousand tax-free Power-Trition kroner, and the whole world was our oyster. When we got back to the flat, we cheered loudly and took turns holding the cheque above our heads. We poured tall rum and Cokes and drank them while we eyed the cheque, which we'd rested against the TV.

"Pinch me, Asger, pinch me," said Waldemar. "Seventy thousand!"

But I was still on the fence about going to Morocco.

"Waldemar," I said, "you can see Arabs here in Stentofte, and we can find a healer for you in Denmark who's bound to have just as good a track record as Torbi – it's crawling with them. Touch healing, crystals, enemas, you can get the lot."

But no, it had to be Torbi el Mekki in Skhirat. Waldemar had enormous faith in that man, despite having stumbled across him by chance on the internet, and nothing could persuade him to try anything else, even though when I googled it I found various alternatives that were more nearby. Then we could use the money for a proper holiday.

"What about this woman from Malmö, the one who's been healing terminally ill people with her bare hands since she was twelve?" No, not her. Waldemar was unshakeable: the man who otherwise wasn't remotely interested in alternative therapies, who had never done any, wanted to go to Morocco. Maybe it was because it was so far away: because miracles could happen when you'd travelled four thousand kilometres, but not when you'd just hopped on the train from Stentofte to see a healer who spoke the same language and breathed the same air, and whose air of the exotic was a sham.

We took the train into town, of course, to treat ourselves – we were going a bit nuts with our wealth. I might have played a part in building these castles in the air, because I didn't contradict Waldemar when he talked about the journey as something that would bring a cure. In the middle of all the dreariness, I've forgotten to say that by this time it had been spring for ages. We were already at the beginning of May, and the summer promised to be good across the whole of Europe.

The train stopped at the main station, and we got off and took the lift up from the platform. I held my breath because it reeked of urine, and when we stepped out into the crowd and I inhaled once more it was like we'd already set off. We bought a bottle of cava at a kiosk and settled down in Ørsted Park to drink it from the paper cups we'd got at 7-Eleven. Waldemar climbed out of his wheelchair, lay down in the grass and rolled a joint.

"Seventy thousand," he said again. He'd been repeating it at regular intervals since Fitzer handed us the cheque. "I think I'll have a leaving do, invite my family round for some food before we set off."

"Sounds like a good idea."

Waldemar passed me the joint. "In honour of the occasion," I said, taking a puff, and rinsed away the taste with cava. When Waldemar took the joint back and sucked the smoke into his lungs, he started hacking loudly and turned white in the face. It whistled when he breathed.

"Are you okay? You look like death warmed up."

"I can't always tolerate the joints."

"Are you having a rough day?"

"Does the Pope jerk off?"

Waldemar poured more cava into the paper cups. "Seventy thousand," he said. "Seventy thousand, Asger."

We ended up with a Volkswagen – a Transporter T4, which we bought from a man in Rødovre. As we stood eying it in his driveway, he piped up.

"I bought it two years ago. That was six months before I got divorced from my wife. I had this idea, you know, that I could break out of the daily grind by fixing up a VW, and then we could drive wherever we fancied. Share a few adventures. Freedom, I guess. But she couldn't give a toss about the Volkswagen and thought the whole idea was stupid. First off she didn't want me spending the money, but I had to put my foot down and say: 'I'm buying this Volkswagen now, and I'm fixing it up and I'm driving off, and it's up to you whether you want to come with me or sit here getting angry and depressed.' Her friend said she was depressed, you see. The doctor said she was depressed. Her mum said she was depressed. And I said she was probably a bit depressed too. Then she got these happy pills, and for a couple of weeks bugger all happened, even though she took them every morning, but then one day suddenly she got better, and the doctor said that too, that a few weeks could go by and you'd barely notice the difference, and then suddenly it would come rushing back, her good mood, and that was when I got her on board with this idea of taking a drive. I said she could choose. We could drive wherever – wasn't there anywhere she'd always wanted to see? So she said she'd like to go to Holland – see the big dikes along the west coast. Okay, sure, we could make a road trip out of that. But she never really seemed quite . . . I mean, she never really gave it a chance, the Volkswagen, and when the happy pills stopped working quite as well – the doctor said that might happen too – it seemed like she regretted agreeing to the trip. No real reason. The woman next door came out while I was doing it up, and said, just for fun like, *Heeeey, could I get a ride in that thing?* So *she* was up for it. I mean, the idea was awesome, basically, just being able to drive anywhere we fancied, 'specially since the kids are grown-up now. And so we finally set off, this was June, and of course the trip went . . . Well, it really didn't work out. I'd been hoping we could rekindle something, but it was like the further we got into Holland the worse it got, the further we drifted apart. But we kept going, we got down there, she saw those dikes of hers, and they were enormous, but to be honest it was crap, really, and then we decided to split up. We decided there's a time for everything."

The man looked down, fiddling a little with the gravel with the tip of his shoe.

"I still cry about it every day," he said at last.

I didn't know what to say, so I stood there gazing at the driver's seat. Waldemar was in his wheelchair, far enough from us that he could get away with not responding. But the silence got too much for me, so I said, "Well, that's a bloody sad story."

"I just have to get rid of it. Too many memories."

We struck a deal.

It was beige, the insides smelled faintly of cigarettes, and the paintwork was in good condition except for a weird dull spot on the bonnet about the size of a football. The gears were tricky when shifting from first to second – sometimes you had to jiggle the tall gearstick around a bit – but otherwise it seemed to run fine. We had faith in the van. It would probably make it to Morocco, we agreed, as we drove it from Rødovre to Stentofte. On the motorway Waldemar took the gearstick, I depressed the clutch and said, "Take it into fifth," and he said, "Aye aye," and shifted from fourth into fifth, and I let go of the clutch and accelerated, and the needle climbed up to 110, and Waldemar said, "It doesn't half eat up the tarmac, our Volkswagen."

"Got that right," I said.

"Do a handbrake turn."

"You don't do bloody handbrake turns in a Transporter."

"Come on, we've got to know what the van can do if we're ever in a tough spot."

"Forget it."

"I'm fucking doing it!" yelled Waldemar, pretending to reach for the handbrake and the wheel at the same time.

"Idiot," I said, laughing. The engine laughed too, and the needle quivered all the way up to 120 as we overtook a Jaguar.

"Eat our exhaust," yelled Waldemar at the Jag. If ever anyone was too big for their boots, it was us.

So we had our VW now, and there was nothing holding us back. Waldemar sent out invitations to a leaving dinner at the flat in Stentofte.

Waldemar's dad and uncle came outside with us to see the van while his mum and aunt stayed at the table. The roast beef hadn't been served yet: it was wrapped in tinfoil and tea towels and left to marinade while the rest of us had a beer.

"You're not worried about leaving this out here?" asked the uncle, walking around and kicking the tyres with the can of beer in his hand.

"I don't know where else to put it."

"Just as long as they don't smash it up like your wheelchair."

"It won't be here long."

"But the wheelchair was only there one night, right?"

His dad leant over the bonnet.

"What's this we've got here?" He rubbed his index finger over the football-sized dull spot.

"We tried cleaning it with toothpaste," said Waldemar. I shot him a sidelong glance, but the adjudication committee ignored the comment.

The uncle, unmoved, launched into a lecture about buying used cars that lasted the better part of ten minutes, while the dad circled around doing spot checks. Then there was something about the rusty suspension, and the uncle demanded the bonnet be opened and said *phew* as he gazed down at the engine.

"Did you put a finger in the petrol?" he asked me, and I told him I hadn't, but that it should all be fine.

"There's no such thing as should be when it comes to used cars," he said, explaining that you were supposed to stick your finger into the petrol, while the dad inspected the spark plugs and shook his head at my simple-minded *should*.

"This is a bomb on wheels, plain and simple," said the uncle at last.

"Yeah, it's a bomb on wheels, Waldemar," repeated the dad, looking at Waldemar.

"It's hardly going to explode in the middle of our trip," I objected.

"You can't bloody know that," said the dad. "I wouldn't even drive to the baker's in this thing. Bloody suicide. How much did you give for this, Waldemar?"

"I don't want to say," said Waldemar. He was trained in this sort of warfare, and didn't want to expose a flank.

"You don't want to say how much it cost?"

"Nope."

The manoeuvre flummoxed them. It was as simple as it was brilliant. The uncle and the dad couldn't stand it, interrogating Waldemar fiercely to make him talk, but Waldemar got cheeky and started throwing out numbers that were either ridiculously high or ridiculously low. "A million," he said, "no, wait, one krone." So they gave up, called him a stubborn jackass and satisfied themselves with having given a verdict that didn't include the price. On the way back to the flat Waldemar lagged behind in his wheelchair, and I walked next to him.

"It's a great van," I said.

"I know that," he said. "The bomb on wheels . . . Now we have a name for it."

"It's da bomb," I said.

When we got back to the flat, the dad said to the mum – but loud enough for the rest of us to hear – "It's a bomb on wheels, and he won't say how much it cost."

"Well, he's got plenty of money now," said his mum.

"What about that roast, then, Waldemar?" asked the aunt, who was standing by the window to smoke.

"It's making itself comfortable in the kitchen. Are you hungry?"

"Yeah, well, getting that way."

Waldemar went into the kitchen.

"Let me lay the table now I've had a smoke."

Waldemar's dad got up and went to the toilet.

"Give me a shout when the food's ready," he said as he passed.

The aunt stubbed out her cigarette and started laying the table. Waldemar was fussing with the food in the kitchen. I helped her set out the plates.

"You have any kids, then, Asger?" she asked.

"No," I said.

The uncle had sat down on the sofa with a new beer.

"You must be the oldest carer Waldemar has ever had," he said.

"And he's had more than his fair share by now," said the aunt. "There was the one called Poul, who sang. He was applying to music college. Always practising and singing the whole time. Waldemar got a bit sick of that, you remember? Some of that classical singing, it was."

The aunt stopped laying the table and imitated Poul by half shutting her eyes and hooting like an owl.

"Yeah, he also sang on the toilet," said the mum. "And while he was riding his bike."

"But you don't have anything on the side?" asked the aunt.

"No," I said again, putting a glass on the table.

"Want to take over?" said Waldemar when I came into the kitchen looking for an extra glass.

"Gladly," I said, and started mixing the chopped chives into the potato salad.

Waldemar sat down in the living room to rest his body.

After standing in the kitchen for a few minutes without doing anything, I took the garlic bread out of the oven and brought the food to the table.

"I think the food's ready," I said.

"Food," yelled the mum, and the dad emerged from the toilet.

We sat around the table. I downed two cans of beer and stayed out of the conversation, which wasn't about anything worth mentioning.

Halfway through dinner there was silence. The dad finished chewing, put down his cutlery and said, "This is the stupidest idea you've ever had . . . Going to Morocco to see a healer."

Waldemar said nothing.

"This healer's taking you for a ride," said his mum.

"Is it your idea?" the uncle asked me.

Before I could answer Waldemar angrily cut across us.

"It's my idea," he said, "it's one hundred percent mine," and he stared furiously into the potato salad without eating a bite.

There was no more said about it.

It struck me later that this must have been the summer Stein Bagger left his family in Abu Dhabi to fly to New York. That it was there he borrowed Mikael Ljungman's Audi S8 and got behind the wheel with his heavy Rolex and his borrowed credit card to drive west. I've often pictured Stein Bagger's square face: him sitting in the leather seat with cruise control and automatic transmission at his disposal, gliding silently across the mildly rolling and winding roads of the North American continent. As he stared into the setting sun, with the torn shreds of trucks' tyres casting shadows onto the verge, he was completely alone. In New Mexico, tumbleweed rolled across the highway as he drove side by side with a freight train. In Arizona, the landscape glowed orange in the dawn, as though it hadn't yet decided whether it would be translucent or take final shape after the invisibility of the night. He drove in the certain knowledge of being absolutely stuck. That there was nothing else to be done. I wonder if he'd been in the desert to bury his assets. If he'd had one final, urgent secret errand somewhere en route before he turned up at the downtown police station in Los Angeles and handed himself in with the words, *I am Stein Bagger. I am a fugitive from Europe and I'm here to turn myself in.* At first I thought he had, but I don't think so anymore. I just think he wanted to take a drive.

We put our suitcases and Waldemar's wheelchair into the back of the van, which was parked outside the stairwell. Waldemar had got the council to install a folding ramp so that the wheelchair could get in without being lifted. Then Waldemar locked up the flat and stood there a moment, staring at the door. I walked towards the van, sensing that he might want to be alone.

"For Morocco," I said, as we sat in the front, then I declutched and turned the key in the ignition, and the engine started. Waldemar said nothing. He simply buckled his seatbelt, smiled and nodded.

The sun was still low, and the day was fresh. The gulls picked at the deserted lawns with their beaks, and the slanting light made the concrete buildings look especially porous.

We were silent across Zealand, and soon we were approaching the area where Yummy Dreams came from. We saw farmyards like empty building sites, a wrecked moped in a ditch and rows of wind-blasted trees. There was no queue at the Rødby–Puttgarden Ferry Terminal, so we went on board and sat down with a cheese and butter roll and a cup of coffee each. Waldemar was pleased that we were one of the first to get a table. Then the ferry set off. A gull stood sullenly for a moment in the breeze outside the window.

"Are you already homesick?" I asked Waldemar, because he was so quiet.

"No, I'm just thinking."

"About Stentofte?"

"No, about something else . . . I think, in the future, people with enough money will be able to live forever."

"Sure."

I eyed myself upside down in the concave mirror of the teaspoon. The vibrations from the engine made the coffee tremble weakly in the cup. I didn't know what to say, so I said that someday the heart would probably always stop beating. It's like a donkey.

"A donkey?"

"I'm thinking of something I saw one time when I was on holiday in Cairo. I took a taxi along a motorway bridge high above the city, and among the cars there was suddenly this donkey-drawn cart that had stopped. One man was hammering the donkey on the arse with a board, while the other one was standing in the front, practically begging it to keep going. He flung his hands into the air and around the donkey's neck and yanked at it, but it didn't budge. It simply wouldn't go anymore. Then we were past it, and there was nothing new to look at. But I've never really been able to forget it, that donkey."

"A donkey on the motorway?"

"Yeah."

"So the heart is a donkey," he said.

"Yeah, that must be the moral."

We drove off the ferry after an uneventful crossing. Then it was goodbye to Denmark. And although it was May and the next few months would get more and more tolerable, and the girls would be wearing fewer and fewer clothes, and there might even be a few summery days in Copenhagen when you could just stroll around and sit at a pavement café and drink a beer and then sit down at the next one and drink another and know that you had nothing to do, and that the evening would be warm and light, the departure was still dominated by the liberating feeling of having escaped the Alcatraz of mediocrity.

I talked as I drove. I told Waldemar about the cafés in Spain, where you could be served by an older gentleman who had things under control, who was proud of being a waiter because it was an important job, and not an angry, overpaid humanities student who'd taken a side gig and viewed customers as an irritation society had for some sick reason decided to plague her with. "In Spain," I said, getting quite worked up, "you sit down at a pavement café and order a beer, and you don't get some totally stale, flat lager – the stalest, most lukewarm, shitty beer I've ever tasted was in Denmark,"

I suddenly shouted, making Waldemar jump, "– no, you get a *caña*, a little glass, with completely fresh and invigorating beer, and it doesn't take more than a couple of minutes to drink it. But then the magic happens, because now you don't have to fight – you sit there in the heat and you've already geared yourself up to fight for the waiter's attention, like in Copenhagen, and then it happens, out of thin air: the experienced waiter has already clocked that you need a new beer and sets it on the table as he passes, whisking away the old glass – they're busy, the waiters in Spain, it's the professionalism, you're their guest, you can't go grumbling about anything or there'll be hell to pay, but in return things are all sorted, being a waiter is their *profession*, Waldemar, just wait till we get down there, you'll see straight away what I mean."

And then we put the ferry terminal behind us and got onto the autobahn. The autobahn, life itself: a network of veins and asphalt arteries, a pulse of steel. Several thousand kilometres long. We were gripped by it, by driving down the autobahn.

"The autobahn, for fuck's sake," I shouted. And Waldemar said, "Yes, man, the autobahn," and started dancing in his seat as he chanted, "au-to-bahn, au-to-bahn."

Now we were on our way.

Because of Waldemar's health we took the drive in short hops, breaking for the night when he or I couldn't take any more, stopping and looking at the sights along the way, which Waldemar looked up in his guidebook from Stentofte Library. In the van he read aloud from them, stutteringly and hesitantly and with such a radically new pronunciation of all the place names that it was more or less incomprehensible. Nonetheless, I think he enjoyed this peculiar form of entertainment, and I hid my irritation. Only if I had a hangover or if we'd argued on the road did I occasionally ask if he could stop reading today, saying that my brain couldn't absorb any more information, and he'd take it well, put the book away; yet he couldn't help himself: thirty minutes to an hour later he'd go back to the book and continue where he'd left off, or at a completely different place.

That the books were borrowed from the library made me uncomfortable, and I realised in one dizzyingly awful moment on our very first day on the autobahn that the reason for my discomfort was that he might never return them: with Waldemar, death was always lurking in the background, if not in the form of the whistling breathing then in the form of a sudden nosebleed or unexpected fatigue, which put him in a near-comatose condition; not to mention his constant pallor or shaky hands. But suddenly death had surprised me and taken up residence in something I could recognise: the library books and their due dates, which could not be kept to.

As for the sights he chose, I must say he had a real nose for bizarre and obscure places. Everything a true lover of culture would have driven long detours to see he turned up his nose at, opting instead for attractions like a fondue museum in Lübeck, a wafer bakery in a half-abandoned village, where we were each given a taste by a fifth-generation wafer baker who looked himself as though he were mostly made of flour, and a rabbit farm, where we saw a rabbit being slaughtered and skinned; and this small sort of thing I found uplifting, because nothing is as depressing as those so-called tourist attractions where, in a kind of collective lack of imagination, we all traipse along simply so we can say we've been there, that we've seen it before we die. Yes, I know that taking digs at tourism is cheap, but fundamentally I'm not saying anything except that I preferred the places Waldemar chose, preferred the total absence of expectation, which in any case suited our journey so perfectly, since the end goal could be nothing but a thundering, disillusioning and life-destroying flop – the healer in Morocco: our final destination, our holy grail.

Waldemar lugged a yellow Netto bag wherever we went. On the ferry he'd kept it on a chair beside him, which was when I'd first noticed it, and he'd been doing the same thing over the next couple of days. I hadn't thought much of it, and didn't want to poke my nose in – if he felt like lugging a bag around, then more power to him. But that afternoon, stuck in a traffic jam on the autobahn, I asked anyway, half distractedly. I had something between my front teeth that I couldn't suck out, and as I was reaching for a toothpick in the glove compartment – where I kept a little arsenal – I caught sight of the bag, which was resting between Waldemar's feet.

"What *is* in that bag?"

"The money."

"The money?"

"Yeah, the money from Fitzer."

"All of it?"

"Yeah. I don't have a credit card. I got them changed into euros."

For a while I contented myself with chewing on the toothpick without a word. I had to collect myself. Then I said, "Don't you think we should put it in the bank?"

"Nah," he said, gazing through the windscreen. He didn't trust banks. And he liked having cash.

We discussed it for an hour while we drove, but he

wouldn't budge. At the same time, I couldn't bear to watch him hauling around the Netto bag anymore, not now I knew what was in it. In the end we found a solution: we divided a good portion of the cash between us, which we carried in our pockets, then we hid the bag with the rest of the money in the back of the van and brought it up to the hotel with us at night. It wasn't ideal. But deep down I had to admit I understood him: it was a nice feeling looking down into the bag at all the cash.

That night at a hotel in Hamburg, he put the Netto bag under his pillow and said, "Now it's finally up to side sleeper height."

We got to Bremen on the evening of the fourth day. We had no GPS, so we entered the city the wrong way and ended up driving into the suburbs. On one street there was a crowd gathered outside a house. They were staring up at something on the roof. I stopped the van and we got out and joined them. They were looking at a monkey. It squatted on the roof ridge like a chimney, its head leaning against its left shoulder and its left arm slung over its head, so that the hand was resting on its right ear. It made the arm look like a frame around the face, which was peering down at the crowd with eyes we'd have been hard pressed to say contained any human emotion. And yet someone in the crowd of onlookers said, "It's scared, don't go any closer, its owner is coming." But I wasn't sure it was afraid; maybe a bit surprised, if anything. Clearly it wasn't about to come down under any circumstances, not even when the monkey's owner arrived with a large cage in the back of a van and tried to lure it down with a banana.

"Move further back," he told the crowd, and a handful of people did, but only a few; most were reluctant to give up their spots in the front stalls.

We learned that the monkey was a Barbary macaque from a small private zoo, where it had been the main attraction despite pulling in only a couple of visitors a day. But now it was sitting on this roof after escaping from its cage – an escape that the owner, who had arrived in the van, swore was a physical impossibility – its value as an attraction had skyrocketed. It was the object of at least forty or fifty people's undivided attention, solely because it was no longer inside the monkey-proof cage but sitting on a roof barely a kilometre down the road. This might be why I read perplexity in its face, which became more and more indistinct as the sun set behind the house, as though it had decided to hit the monkey right on the top of the head. We squinted, no longer able to properly see the animal, and then there was a yell – *it's gone!* But when the sun went down behind the roof it was still sitting there, now even more inscrutable, because it looked as though the whole neighbourhood were on fire – its mysterious and utterly spectacular performance on the roof was set against a backdrop of flaming sky.

It wasn't locked into position anymore with its arm over its head; a bit of life had got into it now. It had started grooming itself, its movements bashful. But that didn't last long. Soon it froze into a new position, while the sky was extinguished into a deep blue, and suddenly the situation seemed so astonishing, with the monkey up there on the roof so alone and so free, and I'm not sure what got into us, whether it was loss, desolation, sadness or maybe even a strange, bittersweet pleasure at its freedom, but all of us fell silent.

It got darker still. And we were still more silent. A man slipped out of the crowd and went into the adjoining house. We noticed him because he was the only one moving. The blackbirds had exploded into song as the sun went down, but now the last of them had finished. I don't know whether it was a change in the humidity, or maybe a breeze dying down, no longer carrying the sound of the motorway, but even the traffic ceased, and there was total silence. When one of the spectators, a little girl, dropped a fork that for some reason she'd had in her hand, the whole crowd jumped as it hit the tarmac, and the mother bent down and picked it up quickly, hiding it in her bag as she grabbed the girl's hand, so embarrassed that she stared stiffly up at the monkey to avoid our eyes.

The man came back out of the house. He had something in his arms. It was about the size of the monkey and glittered in the dusk like the fork, and he edged gingerly through the crowd until he reached the garden gate and went into the empty garden. Still no one said a thing. Only now did we see it was a tuba he was holding. He took up position with one side towards us and the other towards the monkey, and while gazing rigidly at it he put the mouthpiece to his lips. Like some sort of appeal to the monkey to come down to its owner, or perhaps, in fact, to express the wish that it stay up there – who knows, we never asked him – he started to play. An appeal to something it certainly was, that much was clear. He blew sincerely into his tuba without a shred of affectation or falseness, and it got us right in the heart. The monkey, the night and the silence, which allowed the tuba's appeal to spread. I felt that if there'd been anything bogus about his playing, if it had been a display and not an undefinable and incredibly beautiful plea to everybody listening, the silence would have choked any noise that tried to escape the tuba, but that didn't happen; the brass notes were allowed to spread, and they were like small droplets of fluid mother of pearl dripping down a cloth of black velvet, slowly seeping in and disappearing. A cloth of black velvet that spread as far as our vision's edge.

An older gentleman standing next to me cried without a sound. The man with the tuba finished his rhapsody, which he'd played at a slower tempo than I'd ever heard it – it was only many years later that I discovered the piece was by Vittorio Monti and was called "Czardas".

Then the authorities arrived in their cars, and there was a spotlight pointed at the monkey, which got up and started walking back and forth on the roof, unable to escape the swinging beam of light. A tranquiliser dart was fired at the vet's command, hitting the animal in the thigh, where it stayed poking out. After the bang of the rifle it was as though we sank into an even deeper silence than before. At first the monkey sat down on the roof ridge, but then its head sank onto its chest and it tumbled forwards, sliding on its belly down the roof and over the guttering and landing in a bush. Done. When the silence ended, we couldn't get away fast enough.

We worked our way further into Europe. The journey was taking a toll on Waldemar's health. He was forced to spend ages sitting in the van, had to climb in and out and often ended up walking more than was good for him. But, just mentally speaking, driving down a straight road was still preferable to the concrete labyrinths of Stentofte. Did he miss anyone from home? No, he didn't, and nor did I. We both found it easy to let go of other people – or maybe it was other people who found it easy letting go of us? I don't know, but it felt quite natural leaving everything. The silliness of searching for a healer still bothered me, of course, but moving south seemed a thing we took for granted, as though it were happening under the same laws by which a tear runs down a globe.

We travelled with the sense of being forgotten, of being lost to the world back home, of being torn loose from time and space. Yet although I harboured a strange, childish doubt that "back home" even existed anymore, and whether it was even possible to establish a connection to it, I suggested to Waldemar that he should call his family; but he was against it. He'd called once after Hamburg, where the coverage was surprisingly bad, and had a weird, ghostly conversation full of echoes and delayed voices that broke with all rhythm and synchrony.

Sometimes I tried to picture Torbi el Mekki, but I couldn't, and when I asked Waldemar he just said it didn't matter what he looked like. But what I was really asking was if Waldemar thought we would make it down there, because to me it seemed like an unrealistic goal. But I've always been like that. Once I start mulling things over, everything seems impossible – simply opening a door feels like something that shouldn't work in practice. Did Torbi el Mekki even exist in reality, I wondered.

It happened for the first time on a country road somewhere slightly north of the French border. We'd taken a small detour to see the countryside, and the detour had grown and grown until the day was gone and night had fallen.

Now there was a car behind us, dazzling us with its headlights. They shot long beams through the rear windscreen and made the mirrors seem like plates of aluminium burning in acid.

The car didn't keep its distance, instead pulling up very close behind us with its headlights, which seemed even stranger considering it was pitch black, and that there weren't any other cars on the road at all. It bothered Waldemar more than me. He'd been sitting there dozing as we listened to music, but now abruptly he was awake, turning constantly in his seat and peering back into the blinding light.

"Do something," he said.

"What am I supposed to do?"

"Something. I can't take it."

Fine. I signalled and pulled over to let the car pass.

"It's stopping too," said Waldemar. "It's just stopping in the middle of the road and shining its headlights."

"There are loads of idiots driving on these roads, we'll just keep going. Maybe it's someone who's scared of driving in the dark and would rather be right behind us. There could be all sorts of explanations."

"I don't like it."

"Relax. Put a jumper over your head and go back to sleep."

"Not with that light behind us."

"Hmmm."

I depressed the clutch, coaxed the vehicle into first gear, let go of the clutch, hit the accelerator and worked my way back up into fifth, while the light behind us accelerated at the same pace. Waldemar, who really shouldn't have been as annoyed as I was, since after all I was the one driving the van, was for some reason driven absolutely bananas by the light, and after a few kilometres of trying alternately to speed up or slow down, to either drive away from the car or force it to overtake, I stopped again, and our pursuer – because now that was literally what the car seemed to be – stopped too. By now I was keen to put the whole thing behind us, and too annoyed to be afraid.

"You'd better stay here," said Waldemar, but I got out and walked back towards the car, towards the white light that forced my eyes to the tarmac. All the tiny pebbles were as clear as in a flash photograph. Then I heard the car start again, and I walked onto the verge, but instead of passing me it turned around and rolled slowly back down the road.

I watched it drive out of sight. Now I wasn't blinded by the headlights, I could see it was a black Audi. When I turned back, Waldemar had also got out and was standing with one hand on the open van door, gazing into the darkness where the two red dots had just disappeared.

A few days passed before the car with the dazzling lights dropped out of our conversations in the Volkswagen. By the end there was no more to be said, because Waldemar had already said such a tremendous amount about it over the past few days. He thought both that I was lucky to be alive, walking towards the car like that the other night, because there must have been a total psycho behind the wheel with a gun, and also – doing a U-turn – that it must have been someone we knew following us. When I asked who that could be, he said it could be Fitzer, or the caseworker bent on revenge, or a journalist: his appearance on morning television and as the happy handicapped story of the week in the TV guide had gone to his head.

"Or maybe it's one of your old enemies," he said.

"I don't have any enemies of the calibre who'd pursue me through half of Europe," I replied. Okay, but then it was the taxman, and then it was the drugs police, and it got more and more absurd until in the end the only thing he could say with certainty was that he'd felt like someone was trying to choke him when the car was behind us, puffing its dry light in through our rear windscreen. He couldn't describe the terrifying thing about the experience any better than that. An image of the monkey caught in the spotlight inevitably popped into my head. But I didn't mention it. I only said what at that point I believed was true: that we wouldn't be seeing the car again. Waldemar rolled a joint and didn't answer.

We had driven off the main road somewhere in the middle of France. Another one of our detours. Waldemar had seen on a poster at a petrol station that it was Cheese Day at a nearby village. After trying some samples from a booth in the square, we left the village again. One hour later we were lost.

"Why didn't we buy a GPS?" I said for the twentieth time that trip. It was Waldemar who was navigating, and I'd resigned myself to letting him have his way, although I knew very well we were driving in the wrong direction. In my despair over his obstinacy, after a discussion at a crossroads I'd let him decide, and I drove for the next hour without a word, following his increasingly confused and unreasonable directions. It was a peculiar kind of sadism that was meaningless, because I had no hope of making him admit I'd been right at the crossroads. Stupid he was not: when at long last he conceded we were lost, and I said we should have chosen my route at the crossroads, he merely said there had been three roads to choose from, so we couldn't be sure I was right. The right road could just as well have been the one neither of us chose.

Reining in my exasperation, I asked if I could maybe help look at the map, and Waldemar, who was just staring at it without really *seeing* anymore, let me have a glance, but by that time it was too late: we'd driven down so many narrow twisty roads that I didn't have a cat in hell's chance of guessing where we might be on the fucking map either.

We were moving upwards into the mountains. I mentioned we were in central France, but to be precise we were in the region of Limousin, which is apparently one of the most sparsely populated areas in France. We looked for someone to ask for directions. I only spoke a few words of French and Waldemar none at all, but we agreed we could get a person to point out where we were on the map – then we could manage the rest ourselves. We were optimistic after having hatched that plan; now all we had to do was find a stranger and we'd be saved. But we saw no one. The road began to climb steeply, coiling into hairpin bends. I honked as we blindly rounded the rocky outcrops, and to begin with the honking echoed through the lush, evergreen valleys, but as we got further up the air started to condense into fog, which ate the echoes and made it harder and harder to see.

At first the mountains and sky vanished, then the woods and cliffsides, until finally the only thing we could see was a short stretch of asphalt in front of us.

On one side we sensed a precipitous drop into the pea soup.

The Volkswagen fought with the climb: at the sharpest bends I had to shift into first gear, and the engine began to cough feebly with the damp, which seeped in and settled everywhere, and we talked affectionately and pleadingly to it, because this wasn't a place we felt like breaking down. I switched on the fog lights, but it was like shining a light onto a giant pillow. Beneath us the asphalt turned into gravel, and the gentle noise of the wheels gripping the tarmac changed character, becoming crunchier. The windscreen was dripping with condensation, and when the fog began to trickle through the crack at the top and everything started getting clammy, as though we were sitting in a steam room, we rolled the windows up.

And so we climbed, gradually losing our sense of time. Neither of us said anything; it was an odd blend of unease and drowsiness. Our drive through the fog seemed like one long wake-up from anaesthesia. Now and again the whiteness lifted, and we were permitted a glimpse of a shadowy world that did not reassure us but merely increased our unease. This was a blurry, foreign element in which we found ourselves, and we did our best to name the things that fleetingly appeared. Tall, twisted figures stooped out of the turbulent smoke, turning into sentries along the route, which led to a forgotten realm of the dead, monsters from childhood, guests from a nightmare. We had no idea whether they were trees we were looking at – and I'm still not sure they were trees we were looking at. We drove into a massive silence and whiteness, and into whatever might step out of that whiteness. We expected to see UFOs and ancient monsters, our own doppelgängers.

But, at last, the slope began to ease off, and gradually the road flattened and broadened, and now it was safe to park on the verge, so I pulled over and said I didn't fancy going any further in this fog.

"Let's smoke a joint while we wait," said Waldemar, and started roasting a cigarette. He'd brought out a little stash of marijuana that sat in the glove compartment. I'd tried to explain that a customs officer probably wouldn't care that it was for medicinal use, but Waldemar was unmoved; he wasn't about to go running around some foreign city to buy hash, he didn't fancy being that sort of idiot. In fact, it wasn't a little stash, it was a medium-sized stash. Actually, maybe it was a little bigger than medium-sized. I wondered sometimes whether he had some hidden elsewhere in the van, because he didn't seem to be keeping any back, but maybe he just didn't think about conserving it. I'd decided I wanted to clear the decks before we got to Morocco. Once we were outside Europe I didn't want to risk anything.

"I've never seen anything like it. It's like we're in a cloud," I said.

Waldemar lit the joint. I decided to smoke too. We had two air mattresses and sleeping bags in the van, and you could get a good night's sleep in there, so it wasn't strictly necessary to drive much further that day.

We sat and smoked without saying much to each

other. Outside the window it was completely white, but once in a while a bubble of clear air blew past and we could see our surroundings. There were fields either side, though they didn't look like they'd been cultivated for many years. Gradually the smoke made it as foggy inside the van as outside.

"So we're just sitting here," I said to Waldemar.

"Yeah, we're sitting here."

Then, at some point, I must have fallen asleep.

When I woke up the fog had gone, and it was dark. Waldemar was asleep beside me. The van smelled of hash, and I opened the door and got out.

The air was cool and refreshing. Not only had the fog lifted, but there were only a few long, fibrous clouds against a twinkling, crackling soup of stars. The moon was high in the sky, absolutely round and filled with craters, gushing with cold light, so that the trees at the borders between the neglected fields glittered with silver and cast sharp shadows. The silence was colossal, a different clear silence than beneath the fog; this wasn't the deadening of all noise, it was the complete absence of any sound source. I was gripped by an acute sadness. A sense of loneliness. Of having done something stupid. I looked at Waldemar, asleep in the van, and wondered if I should just drive him home now. I was petrified he was going to die on my watch. Maybe it was just the joint putting me in a sad, resigned mood.

Then I heard an engine – it sounded like a moped approaching. I reached into the van and grabbed the map, ready to ask for directions when the vehicle passed.

The noise of the engine grew louder, and soon a little white light came into view. It turned out to be a bike lamp . . . and when it was close enough I could see that it was mounted on a Christiania cargo bike, which was fitted with a VéloSoleX engine on the back wheel.

I waved, and the woman on the bike pulled over. We only managed to exchange a few phrases before she asked me in Danish if I was a Dane.

"Yeah."

"Have you come to visit the farm?"

"What farm?"

"We just call it the farm. We're a couple of artists living in a house nearby . . . I thought you were looking for us, because we don't see many people getting lost up here."

"Um, no. We just took a bit of a detour . . . I mean, we thought we'd see a bit of the area."

"It's just a crazy coincidence, then. That's pretty much got to mean something, right?"

"Yeah," I said, and laughed.

"Whoooo, spooooooky," she said, laughing too. "Must be the fog."

Then she caught sight of Waldemar, who had woken up in the back and was rubbing his face. She waved at him. Waldemar waved back.

"Is he Danish too?"

"Yeah."

"You should drop by the farm. Have a glass of something and say hello, before you drive on."

She started explaining the way, but a moment later

she interrupted herself and said it was too complicated. We should simply follow her in the van – it wasn't more than ten minutes away. Her name was Ida.

We drove after the motorised cargo bike, ending up in a small village. In the dark we could just make out grey stone houses. The farm was five minutes' drive away, down a gravel track.

We parked and followed Ida across a farmyard to a door. I paused, waiting for Waldemar, who had left his wheelchair in the van, and Ida stopped too and looked at him enquiringly. I was about to reel off a few of Waldemar's syndromes as a kind of explanation, but caught myself, and merely said he had a wheelchair in the van, but that he could walk short distances fine if he took it easy.

"Right, sure, well then he should definitely take it easy," said Ida. Waldemar was concentrating on walking, and didn't hear a thing. Then Ida opened the door in front of us, switched on a bare lightbulb in a hallway lined with jackets that hung in clusters on pegs along the walls, took a few steps as she kicked off her shoes, then opened yet another door and shouted, "We've got gueeeeessts."

The room was large and high-ceilinged, with a flagstone floor. Along the long wall opposite was a staircase leading up to the first floor, and to the left of us a door opened onto the kitchen.

A man with a bowl cut was sitting on a sofa, obviously quite drunk. He was the only one in the room. There was a group of empty wine bottles on the coffee table, and the ashtray was overflowing. He had ash all down his front and a cigarette in his mouth. His name was Thorkild, and once we'd sat down with Ida and been offered a glass of wine there was no end to his moaning. He thought he knew exactly who we were, so we didn't need to say a thing. His girlfriend had just dumped him, he made it a point to tell us; she was an installation artist who'd also been living at the collective, but she'd moved to Paris to live with a sexologist called Pierre she'd fallen in love with. She had been stolen from Thorkild in the most shameless and manipulative way. There was a long run-up, which had started with them meeting the sexologist at the premiere of a documentary film about queer theory, and he'd invited her to dinner, and only her, although Thorkild had been standing next to her. He'd served food in a cast-iron pan that was placed carelessly on the table, and she'd been able to talk to him as though to a good female friend, and they'd drunk a load of wine.

"He started ever so slowly to ruin our relationship," said Thorkild, "and I was completely powerless, because I'm no match for that sort of manipulation, I just believe in the good in people. I'm quite honestly too innocent to guard against that type of person – I approach the world like a child. It makes me a fantastic artist, but it also makes me vulnerable to all the scumbags out there. And he kept easing in these little wedges, right from that first dinner – about our sex life, mostly, but he always did it in a way that made me seem paranoid if I tried to do anything about him plotting. The whole time there was this fundamental accusation of egotism and emotional callousness. So I had to sit there and take all these complaints from Caroline that I could hear was stuff he'd planted, of course – it was something about the word choice, different words she didn't need." He paused to take a slurp from his wine glass, then looked straight at me.

"At one point she wanted to fuck me in the arse with a strap-on dildo, and she made no secret that it was one of Pierre's suggestions. She said Pierre thought it would be the only thing that could save our sex life, and she could sit there sprouting loads of university language and be completely serious and negotiate about the strap-on like it was politics she was talking about, and I'd bet my bloody hat Pierre's never been fucked up the arse with a strap-on dildo, that she doesn't fuck *him* up the arse with a strap-on dildo, that it isn't even on the table, and I was stupid enough to go along with it . . ."

"Thorkild, I think you should be getting to bed soon," said Ida.

"No, let me finish, for Christ's sake. Don't start acting like Caroline."

But by now Thorkild was too annoyed and withdrew into himself, scowling from underneath the bowl cut, slurping up more red wine and lighting a cigarette. Now and again he'd give some grunt of displeasure.

Ida started asking us questions. It was obvious she couldn't quite figure out what kind of trip we were on, but Waldemar wasn't stingy with information, and soon he'd told her all about the money from Fitzer and the healer in Morocco.

When I felt that enough was just about enough, I began asking questions about the collective.

Ida said that originally six artists had moved down there shortly after Fogh came to power in 2001. It was his New Year's speech that had been the last straw.

"We felt like somehow we had to mark our disgust with the government, and when they started a war on the country's artists we moved abroad. We simply carried through on the conversations back home. So the farm was actually set up as a protest against the change in the system. We were so ashamed of Denmark that we had to emigrate. It was partly a political happening," said Ida, and kept talking, about politics and art, about new people who had come to the collective, and old ones who had dropped away.

Thorkild had been sitting for a while with his head lolling all the way to one side while his cigarette burned down to the filter in the ashtray, but now his head suddenly jerked upright and he stared at us with wide open eyes that gradually narrowed, and once they'd reached a more-or-less normal size he started talking over Ida, who fell silent and poured herself a glass of wine. Thorkild glowered down at the bottle, paranoid, and was quiet for a few seconds, but once he was sure that Ida was only taking a little sip, and that it was still half full, he started talking again, first about the French sexologist, whom he'd begun calling Pierrot instead of Pierre, and when the rest of us chuckled at the mix-up, which might have been deliberate and might not have been, he shouted that Pierrot wasn't funny. "You can't expose children to a character like that," he said. Personally he'd experienced something he considered a definite assault. It was at the amusement park in Copenhagen, and he was a little boy, and his parents had parked him on a bench in front of a stage where Pierrot was standing, and then it had happened: Pierrot had revealed an egg onstage and cracked it into a bowl and made pancakes out of it and given them to the children, and he'd never be able to forget it . . . the red mouth in the dead white face and the egg suddenly appearing, and the smell of pancakes. I had to agree with Thorkild that it was an inappropriate show for kids, but being right only made him more bitter, and after calling us suckers he fell asleep again.

When I think back to the people at the farm, each one has a distinguishing characteristic that pops into my head and dominates the image I'm trying to recall. Thorkild has his bowl cut, Ida had a downy upper lip, and that that was the first thing I noticed when I saw her climb off her Christiania bike in the moonlight.

Once we'd finished the wine and Ida had had the opportunity to interrogate us a bit more, we lifted Thorkild's legs onto the sofa, took off his shoes and covered him with a blanket, tucking a pillow under the bowl cut.

"Can you share a room?" asked Ida, showing us into a converted barn. The room was furnished with two beds and an armchair in the corner. She fetched us sheets and blankets, and I had to make both my bed and Waldemar's, since he had collapsed in the chair.

"And I hate making beds," I said, but Waldemar didn't respond. He just shuffled like a sleepwalker towards his clean sheets, kicked off his shoes and lay down to sleep with all his clothes on. It had been a long day. I considered sneaking back and drinking the last drop of wine, which we'd left in the bottle on the table, but got into bed and stared at the ceiling for a while instead. Then sleep came prowling.

I was woken next morning by the first grubby light – we hadn't drawn the curtains – so I got up and pulled on clothes from the day before, which I'd chucked on the floor, then went outside without waking Waldemar. The sun was already above the horizon, busily burning off the mist that had gathered all around us in thin banks.

The farm was situated in a bend in the gravel track, and to the rear a lawn sloped down towards a small pond, behind which began the forest.

Standing at an easel by the pond was a man. As I approached I saw he was painting a watercolour. He didn't notice me until I was quite close. I told him I'd met Ida the day before and spent the night there with a friend.

The man's name was Helmer.

"I always get up early to paint," he said. "It's just, you know . . . the light. I'm a bit sick of . . . not really into anything except these, um . . . It's the only thing, yeah, that I . . ."

Then he took his cigarette and tapped it into a thin bluish-grey mixture in the lid of the paintbox, smeared the brush around in it, added a stroke to the watercolour and said, "Done." He had a harelip and the best of intentions, and still bore the marks of childhood bullying in the provinces: although he was in his early forties, it was as though the smell of secondary-school egg sandwiches still hung about his clothes. Since coming to the farm he'd not done anything of note; the idyll had spun him into a cocoon, but under no circumstances did he want to leave, and now he contented himself with going to the pond a couple of times a day and painting a watercolour. It kept him busy. He had a small inheritance. He offered me a cigarette, and we smoked sitting in the grass as we gazed at the water. An enormous beetle had wandered out along a stalk that dangled over the water, and all the scurrying made the tip of the stalk tickle the surface, dotting it with tiny rings. Otherwise the pond was a mirror. A dragonfly patrolled the air above the water.

There were signs of life in the house behind us, and we went up to eat breakfast. Waldemar, too, had got up, and now appeared. A man in a dressing gown came downstairs and took the seat beside Helmer. "Simon," he said, nodding to us and pouring himself a cup of coffee. Thorkild was still asleep, but Ida was boiling eggs, and this had prompted a ritual exchange of opinions between Ida and Karl, who seemed to be some sort of unofficial leader at the collective, about the cooking time of soft-boiled eggs. Karl was nearly six foot six and had a large head, on which his bald crown seemed to dominate the face beneath entirely. Emma, his wife, sat next to him. She was sorting out food for their child, Delfi, who sat at the end of the table and stared mutely round at people. Delfi was five.

"Is Delfi a boy's name or a girl's name?" asked Waldemar, who evidently couldn't tell that Delfi was a boy.

"We chose a gender-neutral name for Delfi," said Karl. And Delfi, who understood what the conversation was about, put his hands on the table in front of him and started to talk. "Nobody's going to tell me if I should be wearing pink or blue."

"No, that's right, Delfi. Or what you should play with."

"No, Emma, nor what I should play with."

Emma smiled at Delfi and put the plate in front of him, and Delfi began with tremendous dignity to eat his food.

"Delfi is a boy," I said to Waldemar, because I could see he wasn't satisfied with the answer and was about to continue the conversation.

"So Delfi is a boy's name, then," decided Waldemar.

Karl glanced at him irritably but said nothing.

"Eggs are ready," said Ida, lifting the saucepan off the hob and putting it under the cold tap.

"You sure about that?" said Karl.

"Karl," said Emma, smiling and brushing a wisp of hair back from her forehead.

Ida served the eggs and sat down at the table with the rest of us.

"Waldemar and Asger are on their way to visit a healer in Morocco," she said.

I felt like an idiot. Waldemar looked unconcerned, and chopped the top off his egg.

"Morocco," said Emma. "That sounds exciting. Are you both going to be healed?"

"No, just me," said Waldemar. "At least I don't think Asger wants to."

"What's the matter with you?"

Waldemar mentioned a few of his illnesses and syndromes, which elicited general sympathy around the table.

"Do you think one healer can handle all those things?" said Emma.

"As long as he can heal a bit, that's fine with me," said Waldemar.

Simon, who'd been eating without a word, got up and said he had something to do, yawned nervously and went upstairs. We heard his footfall above as we fidgeted with our teaspoons in our soft-boiled eggs. Ida told us that Simon was writing essays in his room – political essays. I tried during our stay to coax him into showing me them. I had a suspicion that he just sat in his room and played with himself. It seemed that Politics was a common denominator for all the artists in the collective; even Helmer, if he'd felt like joining in, could have interpreted his watercolours as a political act. Simon's distinguishing characteristic was the nervous yawn, and when I say nervous I'm not quite sure what I mean, except that it was a yawn prompted by something other than tiredness, a kind of tic, a little performance he used to fill any gaps in the conversation.

Karl declared that we could stay as long as we liked. "Plenty of space here," he said, throwing out his arms, and the light flashed on his crown.

We set off for the village, Waldemar and I, to have a little nose around. An old man emerged from the door of a farmhouse as we passed. He nodded to us and picked up a stick, then hobbled over to a dungheap and poked it in, as though trying to take its temperature. Next to the dungheap was a dead pig with its legs in the air, like a pink speech bubble proclaiming that sure, it was pretty here, and the swallows skipped across the meadows, but for insects they were harbingers of death, and beneath it all lurked decay and ruthlessness, the ruthlessness of nature, which was also exemplified by Waldemar, trundling towards the small French village in his wheelchair.

"The liberating thing about nature," I said, "is that it doesn't have good intentions."

"Good intentions?"

"When you want something good. One of the worst things is when people want the best for you."

"Yeah, that always goes wrong."

We moved aside for an old pickup truck that was labouring up the mountain.

"You know what's worst of all?" I continued. "What's worst of all is that people can't see anything without feeling sympathetic. And when they feel sympathetic, they either try to help and make the whole thing worse or they demand that society help. And what society does to help is to oppress everybody except the person suffering, the one who needed help, because society was never capable of helping that person to begin with."

The track sloped steeply. After we rounded a bend, the landscape came into view below us.

"The thing is that we've encouraged sympathy to such an extent that it's become perverted – it's become a mockery of true sympathy, and on the other hand we've forbidden other, equally noble emotions. The thirst for revenge, for instance. The thirst for revenge, which is definitely the most human feeling of them all."

We paused in the shadow of a tree and drank the water we'd brought. The sun already was hammering down around us, and the dawn's clear peal of chilly light and twittering had been replaced by the chanting of the cicadas in a sun-perished landscape.

"Nature is evil," concluded Waldemar. "Nature is evil, and society is evil."

"Yeah," I said. And I continued. Nature was evil because it had inflicted his illnesses on him, and society was evil because it had paid his family to be with him: when Waldemar was little, the council had employed Waldemar's mother to look after Waldemar, and in doing so society, with its sympathy and its money, had put a nasty wedge between Waldemar and his mother, and he only realised it now he'd put some distance between himself and Stentofte. From this distance he could see the indignity and the wickedness, but while society was undignified and hypocritical as well as evil, nature was merely evil, and so nature ended up winning after all, we agreed, and then we reached the village.

People goggled, but only a little, as we arrived in the central square, sweating after the descent. Noticing some sort of café or bar, we went inside to shelter from the sun.

"Let's have some pastis," I said to Waldemar, ordering two, and we sat at a table and poured water from a jug into our glasses, turning the fluid milky.

"Tastes fresh," said Waldemar. "Bet it's good with a joint."

There was sand on the floor – and smoke in the air from a few elderly gentlemen smoking and chatting. Then Thorkild walked into the bar. He carried his bowl cut like it was a pillow balanced on his head.

"Pastis," he said approvingly, going up to the bar to get his own before coming back to us.

He was tired now and instead of talking he listened to Waldemar, who told him what we'd experienced on the journey so far, and said, "Drink your pastis," when Waldemar got too engrossed in the conversation.

Ida came into the bar too, her camera slung over her shoulder, and sat down with us. There were beads of damp on her downy upper lip. The bartender brought her a glass. She took a photo of Waldemar and examined it on the camera's screen.

"You have an incredible aura. Take a look at that," she said, showing the picture to Thorkild and me. It wasn't a bad photo. Waldemar, his dark hair greasy, was staring into the camera with a wholly frank expression. The pastis was on the table in front of him, and in the background, which was blurred and out of focus, the bartender was cleaning a glass. The light came thundering in through the large window overlooking the square, casting one side of Waldemar's face into darkness.

We finished our drinks and went back out into the sun. It felt too hot the moment I stepped outdoors. Together we wandered up the mountain towards the farm. Ida went slightly ahead, and took a picture of Thorkild and Waldemar and me. Thorkild tried hopping on the back of Waldemar's wheelchair so he didn't have to walk, but it started driving very slowly with a sluggish whirr, so he jumped off again. Ida took a picture of that too. She printed it out and gave it to us later that day. I've still got the photograph. Thorkild is standing behind the wheelchair, like the back to a throne. I'm walking a pace or two behind them and to the side, gazing at the landscape with my chin lifted, as though judging it. Waldemar, again, is looking straight ahead, his hand on the joystick of the chair. Thorkild is smiling, but Waldemar has a face like a Native American being photographed by an anthropologist. He'd not been photographed many times in his life, I don't think. There were pictures taken during the media circus that spring, but I'd never seen any photos of him from his childhood.

We ate dinner together around the big table in the kitchen. Emma had cooked. Lamb sausages from the village butcher. Baguettes and salad. The sausages were carried in on a pan, still spluttering in the oil. Emma cut up a sausage into small bites for Delfi and blew on them. Delfi was making an odd warbling noise, like a singer warming up his vocal cords, as he eyed the food. The little plate was set down in front of him, and he began to eat.

"Is it too hot, Delfi?" asked Emma.

"No, it's just right."

Thorkild was a little tipsy. "I've got an idea," he said. "I think I'll make a hotdog." He got up and went over to the fridge, where he found a jar of mustard, then took a bread knife from the drawer before coming back to the table.

"Now watch this, this is how Dad makes a hotdog. Anybody else want one? Simon? You want a hotdog? Waldemar? Asger? Hotdog?"

"Are only the men allowed hotdogs?" asked Emma.

"No, no, everyone can have a hotdog. Emma? Ida?"

"No thanks," said Emma.

"I'll give it a miss too," said Ida.

"Suit yourselves."

Thorkild sliced a piece of baguette slightly shorter than the sausage and cut a groove with the knife so he could open it lengthways. He smeared the insides with mustard and tucked in the sausage.

"It's funny," he said, "about the hotdog's aesthetic. That the sausage has to be longer than the bread. But that's just the way it is – some things you can't mess with."

Thorkild took the first bite.

"Burns like a mother, this Dijon. I can feel it in my nose."

"That's good, Thorkild," said Karl.

"What do you mean?"

"He just means that's good," said Emma.

"Yeah, that's good, Thorkild," said Delfi, putting a piece of sausage into his little mouth. That took the wind out of Thorkild's sails, and he fell silent. I felt sympathetic to his case. It annoyed me, the way they'd said it, *that's good*, and I considered making a hotdog to show my support. Joining him in what was somehow, I sensed, a rebellious childishness. For him, putting the sausage in the bread like that was a battle for freedom.

"We should have had some ketchup and grilled onions," he said, trying to get back in the fight.

"That would work," I said.

"Absolutely," said Waldemar. "And pickles."

"We don't use ketchup here on the farm," said Emma, brushing a wisp of hair away from her forehead.

"It would be a shame for the lamb sausages," said Karl.

"Oh Karl, how could something be a shame for a sausage?" said Ida, laughing, and Karl laughed along, and then Emma laughed too. And Delfi. Thorkild raised his hotdog back towards his mouth.

But as he bit into the sausage the skin burst, shooting a jet of hot fat into his eye. Clutching his eye and yelling, he leapt up, overturning the chair, and rushed over to the kitchen sink. Simon was the first one next to him. "Cold water," shouted Karl. Simon helped him position his head underneath the tap, and Thorkild sloshed water into his eye. Emma fetched a towel.

"Are you okay?" asked Helmer.

Thorkild looked up and blinked tentatively. "I can see out of it fine, it just hurts like hell."

"It's really red," added Emma.

"You poor thing."

Karl took the sausage out of the hotdog bread and held it up between two fingers, inspecting it. "There was a pocket of liquid right here – just look, the skin is all loose."

Helmer came closer and peered anxiously at the sausage, squinting as his harelip quivered.

Thorkild sat back in his chair and poured himself a glass of red wine.

"Could you please stop waving that sausage around, Karl?" he said.

"Oh sure, sure, absolutely," said Karl, putting it back on the plate.

"Ugh, get it out of here," said Thorkild, pushing the plate away and taking a sip of wine.

"Shame it didn't work out with the hotdog," said Emma.

"I don't like hotdogs," said Delfi, stuffing a piece of sausage into his mouth.

After dinner we sat out on the lawn behind the house, chatting and drinking wine. Thorkild drifted away, but the rest of us grouped together. Ida photographed Waldemar without flash in the waning light, making him sit still in the grass because of the slow shutter speed. "Look down towards the pond, like that," she said. Waldemar put a blade of grass in his mouth and chewed it. Then she asked him to take off his T-shirt. He took it off and sat in the grass wearing only his shorts. His ribcage caved inwards; it bore a long scar from the operations. His skin was whitish and seemed parchment-thin, fatless, all the veins clearly visible beneath it. The camera clicked pleasantly. The light was mild. Like fabric softener, it made everything more cushioned. We talked.

Karl and Emma had run a freegan restaurant in Berlin. It was freeganism that had brought them together. Ten years ago they'd met one night by a dumpster behind a Lidl in Prenzlauer Berg. Karl had jumped the fence around the dumpster to see if there was any food in it he could use when Emma popped her head up out of it. "It was love at first sight, in fact," said Karl. They got to talking. They'd both had the sense it was basically impossible to escape the capitalist structures of exploitation – no matter what they bought, they ended up supporting something they didn't want to support. They both felt forced into a vicious cycle of overconsumption and greed, materialism and conformity, and freeganism had been a liberation. It was the principle of refusing to buy anything, insofar as that was possible, of reusing and dumpster diving – basically, stealing food the supermarkets threw out, even though it was fine to eat. "You have no idea what you can find in those dumpsters sometimes," said Emma. "Obviously we demand that everything we buy has to be perfect, so if anything's got a little scratch or a mark, it gets chucked out. Even if food isn't too old, it's discarded because fresher stuff has come in, and people want that instead. One time, Karl found a body in a dumpster."

"That's another story, though," interrupted Karl.

"Yeah, that's another story," said Emma.

Fundamentally, however, it was about a desire to make better use of resources, to work less and stop the money they had earned going to support child labour and overexploitation of the planet's resources, that sort of thing.

After Karl and Emma had known each other a year, they opened Berlin's first freegan restaurant. The prices were low, because the principle was that all the food was scavenged, and all the plates and furnishings were second-hand or junk. They'd actually had a fantastic chef and a little corps of dumpster divers who went out rummaging through the bins behind Berlin's supermarkets at night. The menu depended on what they found.

They hadn't really planned it this way, but the business had actually done very well, and they were able to put money aside. Then, two years after they opened, they had a serious case of food poisoning. Their scavenged food was suspected, and the authorities investigated the kitchen. As it turned out, the chef had had an infected cut on his finger, which had contaminated the food. One of their guests experienced some facial paralysis because of the poisoning, and took them to court. The money they'd put aside during those first two years went towards paying compensation. "I still don't think she can smile to this day," said Emma. It had been a nightmare for them, but it hadn't divided them. They moved on, moving to Copenhagen and living there for a while, but then came the New Year's address. Emma stopped talking. The rest of the story we knew.

Things had lost their colours; there was only dark blue left. It was a warm evening. During the day's sharp sun only the cicadas sounded, but now the whole place came briefly alive before night fell. It was a circus of different noises: insects, birds, the sounds of evening in the village, the wind in the trees, a car driving up the mountain. Thorkild was still keeping his distance. Once in a while during Emma's story we'd seen his figure pop up somewhere in the landscape, walking across a hilltop or emerging from the edge of the forest like a wild turkey, only to glance around and dart back under cover. At one point the bowl cut went waggling along above a row of rosehip bushes, as though someone on the path behind it was carrying a wig on a broomstick. A while afterwards he crossed the lawn between us and the pond, but acted as though we weren't there. By now it was too dark to see where he might be, but it felt like he was still striding around out there, ignoring us, alone with his frustration and his sore eye.

It wasn't until Helmer lit a cigarette and the flame from the lighter created a bubble in the dark that we realised night had properly fallen.

There was something about the farm that made us forget Skhirat. In fact, it made us forget time full stop. Yet while we slept, it came back. I don't know about Waldemar, but that night I had a dream: I dreamed I was carrying plates with meticulously presented French dishes up some steps in an ill-lit stairwell. On the top landing, at least five storeys up, was the healer from Morocco. He sat in a Buddha-esque pose, his legs crossed. His face was missing in the dark, but his hands appeared as he stretched them out to take a dish. Scallops and crispy vegetables arranged geometrically, small rare pieces of meat, a touch of glaze on the white porcelain, a little bed of wheat and something bright yellow. The stairwell was brown and worn, in stark contrast to the cleanliness of the meal. The windows were frosted, but I got the sense it was night outside. There was no climbing down the steps, only the eternal climb up with the full plates, and as soon as the healer had taken the dish in his hands and lifted it to his mouth in the darkness to consume it, I found myself at the bottom of the stairs again, a new dish shoved into my hands by a faceless figure in white. The moment of uncertainty was this, the dishes appearing in my hand at the foot of the stairs. I had no doubt that the healer would keep eating them, but at the same time I knew the appearance of the dishes depended on a very fragile system of cause and effect that I did not understand, and on which even the least disruption would wreak havoc. And if the dishes stopped streaming up the stairs, Waldemar would die. That much I knew.

Next morning, as Waldemar and I sat by the pond and tried to coax a coherent sentence out of Helmer, who was painting what he called his morning watercolour, we heard the sound of the Volkswagen starting. Exchanging a look, we both got to our feet at the same time, while Helmer continued painting, unruffled. I'd started to suspect he was a bit hard of hearing, but in any case the sound of a Volkswagen starting up wasn't something that would disconcert him in the way it disconcerted us. Waldemar came with me for ten metres, but then gave up and sat in the sunny grass while I kept walking towards the farmyard. The Volkswagen wasn't there. When I went out onto the road, I could see it driving away.

I'd taken the Netto bag with the money and put it under my bed, but to be on the safe side I went into our room and checked it was still there. Sure enough, the yellow bag was glowing in the dim light among the dust and fluff. On the table I found a note where we'd left the van keys:

I borrowed your van. Couldn't find you to ask. You left the keys on the table. Back tomorrow at the latest. Needed a change of air.

Best,

Thorkild.

Waldemar was still on the grass.

"Thorkild's borrowed our van," I said to him. "He left a note."

"The money!"

"It's under my bed."

"Thank God."

He plucked a blade of grass and split it with his nail. "But he didn't ask first if he could borrow it?"

"Nope."

"Think he'll bring it back?"

"Yeah, I reckon so . . . Bloody hope so, anyway."

"Well, I guess we're staying here for free."

I sat down next to him.

"Just so long as he doesn't wreck it," he said.

Helmer had taped a fresh piece of paper onto a board and placed it on the easel. Now he was circling it like a bearded man deciding how to attack an ice cream.

"Christ, now he's painting another one," said Waldemar.

"He's unstoppable."

Karl swore when he heard about it, swore and rubbed his bald crown. By now it was afternoon.

"I really am sorry about this."

"Ah, not much you can do about it," said Waldemar.

Simon came downstairs. We were standing in the living room.

"What's going on?" he asked when he saw our sulky faces.

"Thorkild's driven off with the Volkswagen," said Karl.

"You'll never see it again."

"Stop it, Simon, I'm sure he'll bring it back."

"Sure, in six months' time."

Helmer had come in and was hovering by the door, watching the situation in alarm, as though the tension in the room meant he didn't dare step towards the middle of the floor. He slunk along the wall into the kitchen and opened the fridge.

"Could you bring a few beers in here please, Helmer?" said Simon. "We're celebrating Waldemar and Asger staying here a while."

"Sure, but yeah . . . we can't know that, of course."

We heard Helmer shut the fridge. Then he came in with a six-pack.

"I've written four pages of an essay, so I think I can allow myself a stiff one," said Simon. "Four good pages." He yawned in satisfaction.

When I'd walked past his door earlier that day, I'd heard noises coming from inside the room. It had sounded like someone playing *Counter-Strike*.

We all helped ourselves. Helmer sat down on a chair he dragged in from the kitchen. The last beer from the six-pack lingered on the coffee table, reminding us of Thorkild's absence.

Emma and Ida joined us. Emma had been in town to work on a piece. She'd found some plastic army men at a flea market last week. A whole bagful. Small, green men with mine detectors and rifles and hand grenades. Now she'd arranged them on the local First World War memorial and written, "War is real, not a game!" in fake blood on the granite. Ida had documented the happening with her camera. "We're at war out there in the world," said Emma, "and I don't think people get that."

"No," I said.

"Hey, Helmer, you're closest – you mind grabbing a few more beers?" said Simon.

"We'd better have a chat with Thorkild when he gets back," said Emma.

Helmer got to his feet and fetched the beer.

Later that day, as I stood by the window in the living room, looking out and feeling restless without the van, I saw Ida photographing Waldemar again. He was standing in front of his wheelchair with the barn wall behind him. He was wearing only his underpants, and there was a joint in his mouth.

Emma had a piece in an exhibition in a town nearby, and there was a private view two days after Thorkild drove off with our van. Everybody at the farm wanted to go, but only five people could fit in the Peugeot, so Ida took the cargo bike and set off a few hours before the others. Waldemar and I acted as though we were annoyed we couldn't come.

We sat on the sofa after they'd gone. For a while we said nothing – after all the driving, silence wasn't awkward. Waldemar started rolling a joint.

I went out to fetch a beer from the fridge and brought one for Waldemar, but he left it standing there without opening it. Then he had a coughing fit that must have opened a cut in the mucous membranes of his nose, because it started dripping blood onto the table. I ran to fetch some kitchen roll, and he sat holding it under his nose while he waited for it to stop.

"Did any blood get on the joint?" he asked.

"No, not a drop."

I went to fetch more kitchen roll to wipe the blood off the table.

On the whole, Waldemar's uncooperative body had been especially stubborn that day. He always had a little foil pack of pills on him, which gave almost immediate relief to one of the syndromes that afflicted him. I knew the procedure: he'd go white in the face and ask for a glass of water, take out his pills, press one out into a shaky hand and wash it down, then feel better not long afterwards.

The nosebleed stopped, and sure enough he asked for a glass of water a minute later, and I went into the kitchen to fetch it, and when I came back he took his pill. I went to open the window, and looked out.

The sun had gone down, and the darkness sifted down across the landscape like flakes of soot.

A black bird changed position for the night, gliding mutely across the sky with a different determination than during the day. And from the pond, its surface coal-black, giving the impression of endless depth, there was a chorus of frogs. The air flickered as though it were raining, but it wasn't. It squeezed through the window, licked my face and curled around me. The lilacs on the grass billowed like plumes of smoke from a grenade, and beyond that was the treeline, a colourless fringe of darkness, like an upper lip guarding a secret. The lawn was beaten, unpolished silver. As I watched, the pulsing song of the congregation of frogs mingled with the gritty flickering of the night to become one trembling, grey-welded whole: the darkness and its noises were like an inflammation beginning in the eyeball and the brain tissue and settling on the tongue like a coating. Everything outside the farm's diving bell of light now seemed to be formed of black smoke and ash. This was a kind siege. The night was forcing its way into the house.

Regretting what I'd done, I shut the window and fastened the hasp.

Waldemar lit the joint, took a puff and handed it to me.

"Just one puff," I said. I sucked down the smoke and handed it back.

As Waldemar took the joint, he said, "You know, Asger, if Thorkild doesn't come back with the Volkswagen, we've got the money to buy a new one . . . or go by train or something, right?"

"Yeah, we've still got enough money . . . Money's not a problem, as long as you don't throw that Netto bag away . . . But I've been thinking: we could just say that enough is enough now. It's been a fantastic trip, but does it make sense to keep going? What if you get sick or something?"

"Get sick? I *am* sick."

"Exactly. We can see a bit of Spain too, and then drive home. Spain's lovely. But it's probably not a good idea to go all the way to Morocco."

Waldemar stared into space, his lips narrow and colourless. "Traitor," he said. He still had a piece of paper stuck in his nose.

"I'm only saying what I think."

"You can just go home if that's what you want. I'll keep going."

"But why?"

"Because I want to see that healer."

"But *why?*"

"Because I do."

I took up position by the window again. The darkness streamed up from the pond like smoke, creeping over the lawn and sending groping tentacles up to the window. At one point I thought I could see a figure standing with its back to the lawn among the billowing black lilacs, indistinct, like a dream you try to hold onto after you've woken up. When I blinked the figure dissolved into the dark, leaving only the impression of a will out there. That the darkness was alive, and did not wish us well.

We didn't talk much that night, but unlike before the silence was charged.

The others came home later. The wheels crunched on the gravel in the yard, and the beams fell through the window. Delfi was asleep in Karl's arms. Simon and Helmer were half drunk. Emma was tired and happy. She said that Ida was staying overnight in town and would come home the next day on the bike.

Once we'd got into bed, Waldemar said, "So, what?"

"So what, what?"

"Am I going down there by myself, or are you coming?"

"I'm coming."

"You promise?"

"Yes, I promise to come."

I lay there for a while, watching the shadows on the ceiling, while Waldemar's breathing changed as he fell asleep. Now and again his breath rattled slightly, but then found its rhythm again. We said no more about turning back.

Two days later Thorkild turned up with the Volkswagen. He arrived late afternoon like a thunderstorm in August, bringing three hitchhikers with him.

First of all he started setting bottles out on the table, and after an hour and a half he was drunk. We didn't mention the Volkswagen; we were just glad to have it back. The three newcomers sat round the table too, drinking with him. Waldemar and I kept them company. Simon came down, drawn by the hullaballoo. Likewise, Ida. Karl and Emma stayed upstairs with Delfi. I assumed they wanted to avoid the group until the following day, when I sensed Thorkild was in for a rebuke. We saw neither hide nor hair of Helmer, either.

Andrew and Dominique were boyfriend and girlfriend, and came from Australia. They'd been travelling around Europe for a couple of months. In Marseille they'd bumped into Malina from Poland, who had spent her summer holiday drifting around until the money she'd brought from home was spent. Now she was hitchhiking, accepting any offer if she met someone who'd give her a meal. I never got a handle on where they'd met Thorkild. Or where he'd been, or what he'd been up to – he was like a stray dog in that way.

Ida put music on. Andrew grabbed a bottle from his rucksack. Thorkild started lecturing, but was still in a good mood. He'd reached the phase where he'd stopped listening, but wasn't yet coming out with bitter diatribes.

Waldemar rolled a joint. He stuck two pieces of Rizla together to make an extra-long one.

"That's the longest joint I've ever seen," said Simon.

"It's a two-sheeter," said Waldemar.

Simon was delighted; he translated the expression for the guests while Waldemar mixed the hash with the tobacco from the two cigarettes he'd roasted, then poured it into the long tube of paper.

It was always a risk taking a puff of Waldemar's joints, because they were full of lumps – there was a certain slipshodness to his joint making, and he didn't always crumble the hash evenly. When it was passed around, I fell backwards onto the sofa after the first inhalation: I'd run straight into a clump, and sank onto the cushions as though into a bog. The walls throbbed with a slow pulse. Thorkild's barmy head appeared in my field of view, and he poured more booze into my glass, and the two-sheeter continued its tour around the table while the bog water closed over me.

I remember the conversation filled me with a deep

sense of irritation, although it sounded like it was coming from very far away. It was the usual backpackers' chat. Anecdotes and loose facts about languages and countries. About the Danes, who were good at English because of American films that weren't dubbed. About how good at languages the Dutch were too. About how big Australia was.

At some point Andrew orchestrated a drinking game, the rules of which I didn't quite understand. It ended with us drinking pure alcohol. Absinthe and vodka shots. The absinthe we drank without water or sugar or anything – that was how Simon thought it ought to be drunk – and it stung my throat, almost like it was evaporating on the way down.

Malina asked what Waldemar and I were doing at the farm, and Waldemar explained about the trip. A little way into the story, which as far as I could judge was pretty incoherent, he said we had a whole bag full of money. We had money coming out our arses.

"Really?" said Malina.

"We got it from a guy called Fitzer."

"Fitzer?"

"He became a millionaire by selling health foods and sponsored our trip."

"Cheers to Fitzer," shouted Thorkild. "Cheers to that sick arsehole Fitzer."

Fighting my way out of the swampy sofa, I reached for my glass and toasted with the others. "To Fitzer," I mumbled, and we drank. And then I said we should toast someone called Håkon.

"Who is Håkon?"

"He's an even bigger arsehole. He got me fired, and now he's building a mountain in Herning."

We all laughed. It struck me that everyone was laughing hysterically all the time that night. We toasted. I grabbed a bottle of booze and had two quick shots one after another. Ida fetched her camera and started taking pictures. The lens pointed in all directions, and the flash went off like slaps.

"I've taken some fantastic pictures of Waldemar, actually," she said. "He has an incredible aura." Malina leant over, and Ida showed her some of the portraits on the camera's little screen.

"It is really awesome pictures," said Malina in her broken English.

"Handicapped is the new black," said Thorkild.

"Oh, stop it," said Ida.

"Stop what?" said Thorkild.

"Stop being malicious. You're just jealous because Waldemar is so photogenic."

Waldemar, a master of indifference, was entirely unmoved by the conversation. Sometimes I couldn't tell if he wasn't listening, didn't understand or simply didn't give a shit. He was rolling another joint.

"Is that one also a two-sheeter?" asked Simon.

"Yep," said Waldemar.

"Shit, man," said Simon, and everybody laughed again.

Waldemar lit the joint and blew a big cloud of smoke. Ida took a picture.

"Take a picture now," said Malina. She got up, stood in front of Waldemar, bent down and started French kissing him. Ida took another photo. Andrew and Dominique laughed. Thorkild overfilled our glasses; liquid poured down the sides. I drained my glass and got up with a jerk, staggered over to the door, through the hallway of empty jackets hanging on their pegs, and out into the farmyard. The air felt like a damp cloth on my forehead. The music, muffled, was still audible from inside the bright living room. I lay down on the grass in the middle of the yard and gazed up at the starry sky, trying to concentrate on making it stop spinning. I thought moths had eaten holes in a big, black canvas, and that there was light behind it, leaking out, but then the light turned into fine, slow-poured sugar and my eyes were mouth holes, and I could taste the stars, and then I fell asleep.

The birds were singing and the sun shining on my face when I awoke. Waldemar was standing over me, like a black outline in the sun.

"Malina's taken the money," he said.

I sat up. There was a thrashing in my head, as though my brain was struggling with tremendous inertia and could barely keep up with my skull. I threw up between my own legs. A thread of mucous dangled from my nose, stretching all the way to the splatter of vomit before it burst. My eyes were watering.

Waldemar collapsed onto the grass. "Malina's taken the money," he said again. His face was white as paper, and his back was rounder than ever. His arms were limp in the grass between his spread legs.

"What happened?" I asked. I remember picturing Malina just sitting somewhere with the Netto bag clutched in her arms, so drunk she didn't want to give it back.

"Well, she came back to our room, and I showed her the money, and then I fell asleep because of all the alcohol, and when I woke up the bag was gone."

"Where is she?"

"She's gone."

"Yeah, but has she taken the van or what?" I glanced around. The light seared my eyes, everything was white, but both vehicles were still in the farmyard.

"No, she must have walked."

"And you're sure she's not still here?"

Climbing to my feet I walked towards the house, opened the door and shouted her name. Emma, standing in the kitchen with Delfi, shushed me. Andrew and Dominique were still asleep on the sofa. Dominique opened her eyes.

"Where's Malina?" I asked.

"Haven't seen her since yesterday," she said.

I went upstairs and shouted, flinging open the doors of all the rooms. Simon was at his desk, masturbating. Ida was in bed; she didn't even wake up. Karl was in the bathroom, shaving his head. Malina wasn't anywhere. I lurched back down the stairs. The hangover was giving me tunnel vision.

"What the hell is going on?" said Emma in the

kitchen, brushing the wisp of hair back from her forehead two times in a row.

"I've got to find Malina."

Waldemar was still sitting outside. As I staggered towards the barn, he stood up and walked with me.

"I want to get out of here. Let's pack up and drive off and find her."

We stuffed our things into our bags, carried them out to the van and pushed the wheelchair into the back. "I'll kill her," I said.

Emma appeared in the doorway. She was holding Delfi by the hand, and they both looked at us, and I looked back with vomit on my face as I slammed the door after Waldemar, then ran around to the driver's side, got in, started the engine and drove out onto the road.

"She must have gone downhill," I said, setting off towards the village. "She can't have got far."

We raced into the village, across the square and around the small streets, stopping and calling out the window at various people to ask if they'd seen a girl from Poland called Malina; we drove half an hour down the mountain, turned the van and drove back up, through the village, past the farm and ten or twenty kilometres further up; then we turned and came back down. We passed the farm one final time. Helmer, walking across the yard with his easel, neither heard nor saw us. Ignoring my thirst, headache and nausea, I tried to make my vision work properly. Waldemar was slumped into his seat, in one of his semi-conscious states. The feeling that it was him and me against the rest of the world had never been greater.

I must have been doing well over a hundred on those small winding roads, stone houses and scrubby trees whizzing past on the periphery. I was still drunk and high, and I think if we'd found Malina I'd have run her down with sheer fury and hatred. But we didn't find her.

By now it was late afternoon. We stopped at a petrol station further down into the valley and bought two Cokes. I gulped mine down in one long go and got the hiccups, bringing up sweet foam into my mouth. Waldemar remained in his seat.

"Why don't we go back to the farm anyway?" I asked Waldemar. "Malina's gone. You need some rest."

"No, we'll keep going," said Waldemar. "Fuck the farm."

"We won't get far without money."

"Shit," he said. He looked down at the seat between his legs. "What are we going to do, Asger? Tell me what we should do. Can we call Fitzer?"

"No, we can't bloody call Fitzer."

"There's got to be a way."

"Have you got any cash on you?" I asked.

"Yes," he said, "there's some in my bag."

"Good. I've got an idea," I replied.

"What sort of idea?" said Waldemar. There was so much confidence and hope in his voice.

"Monaco," I said. "Monte Carlo Casino. We'll drive to Monaco and win the money back."

Regarding Monaco: one time I was wandering around all alone in a forest somewhere in Scandinavia and came across a little copse of birch trees. I'd been lonely for a while, and so as not to completely forget my humanity I picked up a thick branch, planning aimlessly to hit something. A dead birch tree, not much taller than myself, took the first blow. It turned out to be completely rotten and crumbling, collapsing in a heap of brown dust and flakes of white, dried bark at the first touch. Monaco was the same. Monaco was disintegrating – you could see it in the figures hovering around and the houses' façades, and sense it in the underlying mood of the city. As we advanced into the city it never opened before us; it was like a labyrinth in three dimensions: we drove around at length through a jumble of worn buildings and steeply sloping one-way streets before we finally reached the water and parked the Volkswagen.

The sea was leaden grey and heaving, rubbing up

against the brickwork that dropped abruptly into the water from the promenade. A whitish haze sucked the colour out of the sky and veiled the horizon. Behind us, Monaco rose up into the mountain like a wall of cramped buildings. Stacked nougat houses and palms and glass. It struck us that there was a loose connection in Monaco, a short circuit that manifested in an atmosphere of shabbiness and decay: Monaco's essence was decay and bad taste. Nothing aged gracefully. And as we walked along the harbourside promenade, we saw only the elderly, no one young, as though this were a place people came to get bored and die. Everything moved slowly. The birds, the people, even the cars: Porsches and Ferraris glided past in foolish silence. Slowly, yet thoughtlessly. An older couple came walking towards us, and I fixed on the woman in particular. She seemed as fragile as a blown-out egg, her skin draped over her like a creamed brown cloth, and everywhere there were diamonds glittering, contrasting unpleasantly with her mortality: the stones that could cut glass and the muscles wasting gradually beneath the slack skin. The promenading couple seemed to step out of the warm air like two ghosts, whose curse was to haunt the promenade with their dragging steps and rattling jewellery. Monaco was a ghost town. We found a café where we could wait till it got dark, and spent the money on two cups of coffee. I'd brought a suit, which I now found the opportunity to put on. Waldemar had borrowed a light blazer from me. I smelled of sweat and an old hangover beneath the clean clothes. We hadn't washed since the farm. The money was in my inside pocket.

"Did you at least fuck her?" I asked Waldemar.

"No. I slept."

The pleasure boats in the harbour had looked like large shiny white pills. We saw them from high up in the mountain when we arrived, and as we stood in front of the Monte Carlo Casino, the soft, kittenish darkness nestling warmly around us, the first thing we saw were the glinting cars parked outside the wide steps, and they reminded us of the boats in the harbour. The coloured lights on the façade of the casino drew strange patterns on the paintwork. An Aston Martin pulled up outside the door with a low growl and a valet appeared at once, opening the door for a woman in high heels and a short man in a beige suit and red shoes. Another valet backed the car into place in front of the casino, an impressively effortless piece of parking. The car that attracted the most attention was an Audi S8. It was the only one not sparkling warmly in the lights, seeming instead to radiate darkness and cold. All its curves were perfect, and its silent, stark beauty made the other cars seem ridiculously flamboyant.

We couldn't get up the wide steps to the main entrance and had to go in through a side door to bring the wheelchair. Inside we sank into a carpet, paddling through red plush in a world of crystal and gold, till we arrived via echoless corridors and rooms with glittering bars into a large hall of gambling tables.

For the money we had left we exchanged a little under two hundred euros in chips.

Settling against the wall, we watched and plucked up our courage.

"Roulette is our best chance," I said.

Nobody was having fun at the Monte Carlo Casino. Old men sat at tables empty-eyed, while their younger wives came and went with drinks in their hands. In the corner a man in his thirties had reserved a roulette wheel to himself. It was cordoned off with a rope, and people had gathered to watch. His jacket pockets were full of big, square thousand-euro chips, and he was gesticulating frantically. When the roulette wheel whirred he sang a French song, even trying to make the bystanders join in. He was the only one who looked to be having fun. And even then not really.

"What's he singing?" asked Waldemar.

"No idea."

In an adjoining room there was a restaurant. Occasionally a waiter would emerge to ring a little gold bell, and a couple would head towards the restaurant. On the balcony, people were smoking and gazing out over the sea.

"We can't keep putting it off," I said, tugging the cuffs out of my sleeves, and we set a course to the nearest table. I was ill at ease in the casino, but Waldemar's hardened unself-consciousness was working here too, and he led the way. The wheels drew two parallel lines in the carpet.

He must have been sitting there the whole time, but it wasn't until we reached the end of the table that we saw him.

He had one of the long sides to himself, and around him eddied a smoky darkness, swirling slowly and obscuring his features. On the opposite side of the table sat a Japanese couple and a man in a tweed jacket with a gold tortoise fastened to the lapel. Also on that side was a young woman who wore her hair swept up except for a single long curl, which fell across her forehead like a dividing line between yin and yang, but none of them paid any attention to him. It felt like he was invisible to everyone but us. He didn't play but merely watched, while his fingers toyed with a chip, letting it somersault over his knuckles. The wheel was spun and the croupier let go of the shiny little silver ball. Meanwhile everyone was quiet. It darted eagerly around before falling still. A scoreboard showed black 10, and one of the employees scraped in the chips with the rake and pushed little stacks of winnings over the table. The whole thing took place in silence.

We had no strategy. I had some idea about beginning by betting on either red or black to try and increase what we had to play with and then betting on the numbers.

"Let's start with putting twenty euros on red," I said.

"It's him," said Waldemar.

"Who are you talking about?"

"It's the guy from Martha's funeral."

Waldemar's voice was bright with terror. He was sweating dark stains into my blazer, staring at the figure at the table.

What I remember is the chip dancing ceaselessly over the fingers of a chalk-white hand, which seemed to be reaching out of the darkness with a gesture of invitation. And then came the sound of that laugh, the same laugh we'd heard from the back row in the church.

A whisper across the table: "Number 31". Afterwards I wasn't sure if he'd even spoken. If the dry whisper was only in my head. It was friendly and evil at the same time. Low and yet impossible to miss.

As the croupier spun the wheel and set the ball moving, Waldemar said, "Do it."

Leaning across the table, I placed our stake on the green cloth. All our money on one pocket. My hands shook, and I fumbled with the chips, so the pile ended up slanting steeply. The man rose and walked towards the exit. As he slipped past, I caught a breath of chilly, musty air in his wake, like the caress of dead hands. The wheel was still spinning. The ball scurried like a little steel fish. Blood drained from my head. It was the exhaustion, the hangover, the fatigue. I had the feeling of tipping backwards into a bubbling farewell: things were shooting away from me as though I were sinking, drowning, staring up at a vanishing surface, beyond which shades of red and green sailed in the muted light. Was there chalk in the water? What was this whitish haze drawing a veil over everything? Had the noise of the roulette wheel stopped? Why was it so hard to distinguish it from the rushing in my ears?

I fought my way back to the world in one long, vertiginous breath, and the first thing I saw was that the people around the table were staring at Waldemar. The woman with the curl of hair on her forehead formed words with her lips that didn't come out, and when I glanced down at him, supporting myself with one hand on the varnished edge of the table, his face was whiter than I'd ever seen it before – bluish, like whey or thin milk. Bending down to find his eyes, I asked if he was okay. He said nothing, just opened his mouth and gasped like a fish.

Patting down the outside of the blazer, I felt something in the inside pocket, took out the blister pack and pressed a pill out of one of the plastic bubbles. He held out his hand and took it of his own accord, which was a good sign, raised it to his lips, crushed it between his teeth and swallowed. When I turned around, a tower of chips was being pushed towards us. The scoreboard showed black 31.

We got back thirty-five times our original stake. We exchanged the chips for cash and left the Monte Carlo Casino. A little while later we were in a hotel room. Waldemar wasn't in the mood to celebrate. "It was random," I kept saying. But every time I thought of the figure, I got gooseflesh.

Afterwards we didn't talk much about it. Neither of us could explain it, and it frightened us to over-scrutinise it. I think I convinced myself it had happened some other way than I first thought. I tried selling this line to Waldemar too: I said I'd been thinking of playing number 31 even before we reached the table. I asked if he could remember what the man looked like. "Describe him to me," I said challengingly one time when he came up in conversation, and Waldemar could not. "Did you say the number out loud? No, right? You didn't say 31, you just said, *Do it*. And so I put the money on the number I'd been thinking of playing the whole time. Then you decided you'd been thinking it yourself."

Waldemar found the lie soothing. He never fully bought it, but at least it made him doubt himself, and that was a welcome relief.

We drove towards Spain. The Netto bag we'd exchanged for a white, red and blue bag from Carrefour. In fact, we had to use three bags, one on top of the other, because they were easier to see through.

Most of Spain we did in one long, eventless stretch, no detours or interruptions, and in this way we arrived at sun-racked Andalusia. We couldn't get over the shadows of the orange trees. They lay on the ground as though cut out of black cardboard. Sharply drawn and fresh, in contrast to the trees, which were drowning in dust and sun. Although we'd come too late to see them bloom and too early for them to bear fruit and spread the scent of oranges through the streets, we drove into Seville anyway, where we spent four days. We slept till afternoon and went out at night when the streets were cooler. We drank cañas and ate pork cheek, and the service was impeccable. We saw a bullfight. Now it was the sun in the arena we couldn't forget, the orange sand and the sharp shadows and the crowd that could be both utterly quiet, so you could hear the bull breathe, and run riot with applause. The killing of the first two bulls was disgraceful to watch. It was ugly bullfighting. I felt bad about having dragged Waldemar along, and the audience sulked. The dead bulls looked like enormous rats, leaving greasy streaks of blood in the sand as they were dragged out on their backs, pulled by horses. The third matador was the youngest. The bull was weakened, ready to be killed as it approached him with its head lowered. He went up onto his toes, leaning forwards over the bull, and stuck the sword in; but as he let go of the hilt the bull tossed its head and its right horn caught his side. He was flung up and over its back, landing behind it. The whole thing happened in the blink of an eye. People screamed. A lady next to me grabbed my arm and squeezed it hard. The bull charged straight forward, stopping just as the matador got to his feet. I expected his guts to come spilling out of a gash in his belly, like some strange caesarean birth – that they would land on the orange sand and he would die, but he signalled to the two banderilleros coming to help him to keep away; the horn had only snagged his clothes.

Silence again. The bull, still facing away from him, the end of the sword still poking out of its back, was breathing hard, its ribcage stretching. It got down onto its front legs first, as though it wanted to rest, then rolled onto its side and lay unmoving. Then the noise began. Everybody got to their feet. The brawny señor next to Waldemar waved his white handkerchief and shouted,

"Toredo! Toredo!" Everybody shouted, "Toredo! Toredo!" Everybody waved white handkerchiefs. As always, there were five bulls due to die, but bull number three was the only one we really remembered.

The day after the bullfight we left Seville, and not long afterwards we ran out of road in Europe. The prelude to our voyage, however, was a farce. We arrived in Gibraltar, passed through border control, and drove across the little landing strip situated on the only flat patch of land directly between the border and the city. We parked the Volkswagen, found a place to eat lunch and paid a local guide to drive us up to the Rock of Gibraltar. It quaked like pudding in the shimmering sun, and on top of it there were monkeys. They turned out to be macaques. The biggest one, an especially malevolent specimen that bore a certain likeness to Håkon, reached down from a branch and plucked the bucket hat off Waldemar's head, putting it on his own. We let him keep it – there wasn't much else we could do. He bared his sharp incisors. At the foot of the Rock was the Strait of Gibraltar. We could see Morocco, a thin strip on the horizon. Yet when we got down and tried to buy tickets for the ferry, it turned out we couldn't bring the van. It wasn't a car ferry. Waldemar looked up at me as though it was my fault.

"Don't give me that look," I said.

"I didn't say anything."

"Don't give me that, either."

We had to go to Algeciras. Waldemar groaned when the man in the ticket booth mentioned the name, but it turned out to be just forty-five minutes away. Only a few hours later the Volkswagen was parked in the belly of a ferry while we stood on the quarterdeck, observing the white wedges of foam in the water and Spain shrinking.

"I liked that bucket hat," said Waldemar.

Waldemar's supply of hash, by the way, we'd left on a bench among the rocks of Gibraltar. About five grams was left. We were hoping the monkey with the bucket hat would find it and eat it. So, as we headed into Tangier, it was with a clear conscience.

We drove out the bow door and through customs with no trouble, landing straight in the middle of something I wouldn't hesitate to call a shambles. Everybody wanted something from us, wanted to know where we were from and what we were doing, what we were called, and what kind of hotel we were looking for. I continued in first gear, while people banged on the windows and yelled. One man hung onto the bonnet, waving a laminated piece of paper, while another tried to stuff a brochure through the crack in the window on Waldemar's side. When it was halfway in, Waldemar rolled the window all the way up, so it got stuck. Then, suddenly, we saw the world's fattest woman ascend into the air: seated on the back of a camel that was trying to stand up, she glowed as white as risen dough gone amok. In her hand was a yellow sunshade, its harsh shadow no more than a dot on her bulky body. The camel's eyes bulged, its tongue lolled out of its mouth, and as soon as it had finally struggled to its feet she began slipping slowly to one side. A panic-stricken man tugged at the camel's reins, and it lay down again just as the woman slipped all the way down off the saddle and vanished sidelong into the crowd. We saw a figure grab her parasol; we saw another beckoning to a boy, who came running over with a hand truck. Two dogs followed him, barking.

To the left was a broad beach and a turquoise sea, its shallow breakers lunging forwards and withdrawing at an urgent pace, and the sand was alive with black thronging dots: people darted into the water and back out again, interweaving frantically and spasmodically, opening sunshades and erecting them, folding deck chairs and moving them, and the whole chaotic circular dance appeared to us to be driven by the white sun, like an animal trainer whose whip-like rays could make things vanish into glittering, dazzling nothingness.

We got through the introductory hordes without being hustled – other tourists weren't so lucky, especially those who had to leave the ferry on foot. Pure cannon fodder.

The name, Tangier, had now been stripped of any fascination and mystique, ousted by unpleasant images of the degradation tourism brings with it like a virus. Yet although most places can't live up to their names, there's always something intoxicating about movement. All of Africa was open to us, I said to Waldemar – roll it around on your tongue, Africa – and Waldemar repeated it, and it was as yet unexperienced and intangible and exotic, because it was so big. There were so many places we hadn't been, and where things might be as in our dreams. There were places entirely without names, and brief flashes when the whole thing was so clear it seemed impossible you could ever forget it. And nobody forbade us from driving, just driving. It was in that mood we left Tangier.

But the crossing also marked a transition in our journey. The fact that we were now on the same continent as the healer, it occurred to me, involved an unpleasant duty to reality. And the doubts I'd had, the suspicion that he didn't exist, would very soon be disproved.

I've forgotten the name of the next town, but our hotel was on a street of shops selling car tyres. In the building next door was a brothel. We ate dinner on the roof of the hotel, where they'd set up tarpaulins for people to sit under. We had the chicken. The man who brought our food was communicating with a person through a hole in the wall of the brothel. He winked at us every time he did so. There was no one else in the restaurant. "One of the girls," he said, pointing at the hole and winking. After we'd eaten, we each ordered a beer, taking it over to the edge of the roof and gazing out at the view. The town wasn't big; we had no trouble getting a clear overview. Above the roofs was a multitude of swallows, all around were yellow and ochre fields, and to the north there were several small towns. Gradually, as the sky turned navy, electric lights appeared dot by dot in white and yellow, and we thought we could see the lights of Tangier trickling into the northern sky.

The tyres were tightly stacked outside the shopfronts along the street, leaving barely enough space for a car to drive through. It looked like people were flanked by dark hedges. The asphalt was silver in the light of the street lamps.

Above the muttering din of the city rose a clear flutelike note. It sounded like a large bird trying to imitate the swallows' sharp-as-steel song, which earlier in the day had rained down on the roofs, dying shrieks like plunging suns.

The men came out of the shops and stairwells and stood in their doorways. Leant against the stacked tyres. The hotel employee left the communication hole he shared with his friend and went to peer into the street. Heads appeared in windows.

A man came round the corner with a metal flute in his mouth. He blew rhythmically as he walked. There was no other sound. Behind him came a row of women, probably five of them, and behind them another two men in the uniform of the town: loose-fitting trousers and a shirt that hung untucked. Their shadows were short and diffuse. The man played one last note and turned into the gate of the neighbouring house, where the brothel was located. One of the women had stepped in a puddle of oil and was treading dark footsteps down the street. When the last one had disappeared through the gate, it was like the lid had been taken off a pot, and the sounds began again. "New girls," said the man beside us, winking. Then he dashed back to his hole and peered inside, said something but got no response, and ran down the stairs. A bulky man lifted a tyre off one of the stacks and started rolling it down the street. We sat down at the table with our beers.

Waldemar's chin dropped to his chest and he sat motionless for a few minutes, his breathing raspy. When he lifted his head once more, he took the blister pack out of his pocket and pressed a pill into his hand.

"Want me to get you a bottle of water?" I asked.

"No, no, I'm fine with a beer."

He washed down the pill and smiled at me with dull eyes.

They came from the Ukraine and had flown from Kiev to Rabat with Air France. In Rabat they'd rented a car. Sergej drove and Olegsander lay across the back seat with his brace. Sitting opposite us on the hotel roof, they told us the story. They'd arrived half an hour after the parade of whores, and the employee had served them chicken and put several beers on the table, and gone to speak into the hole a few times and winked at us. Sergej and Olegsander were on their way back to Rabat to drop off the rented car and fly home, but they'd got lost and ended up here, a good way west of Rabat, where they bumped into us. It was a strange coincidence, but stranger things have happened. And, of course, ordinariness implies that the extraordinary happens too.

Sergej and Olegsander were brothers, and it was their Uncle Bogdan, trained as a blacksmith, who had forged the brace that held up Olegsander's head and fixed his arm in place and protected his chest. The whole family had clubbed together to pay for a plane ticket so that Olegsander could be free of his brace. Uncle Bogdan had slowly added to it as the syndromes worsened. The first splint, the one on his forearm, had been made five years ago, when Olegsander was fourteen. Then the splint on his upper arm, and Uncle Bogdan had constructed a moving joint so that the elbow could function; but a year ago he'd welded the joint in place, because bending his arm caused Olegsander too much pain. That day Uncle Bogdan wept as he welded. When Olegsander's head had started dangling, making him scream in agony, Uncle Bogdan, in consultation with the doctor, had fixed his neck in place too. Every day they were grateful for Uncle Bogdan's ingenuity and talents, which enabled Olegsander to move around a bit despite everything, and meant he didn't have to lie in bed all day. His ribs also gave him trouble, and the leather belt around his waist – connected by a rod at the back to the structure that kept his head in place with a kind of metal halo, from which six rods were attached to a harness fitted around his skull – could also serve as the basis of a metal lattice around his ribcage, protecting it from impact. For his ribs were liable to disintegrate like dry bread, and one knock or unlucky movement would be enough to leave his organs protected by nothing but crumbs. Olegsander's right arm was free of the lattice; there the bones were still strong. He reached out and grabbed the beer his brother handed him, and took a sip.

"Soon everything will be different," he said. "The day after tomorrow, when we get home, Uncle Bogdan will remove the brace."

Sergej smiled at him, with a gaze full of love and sorrow. I imagined Uncle Bogdan standing by in some windswept province of the Ukraine, with his welding torch and his tools and his stock of stainless steel. As yet he didn't dare be happy.

But why couldn't they remove the brace now?

We got an answer. Olegsander whispered it, like a secretive spider in a web of steel, which glinted in the moonlight that poured over him through a rip in the tarpaulin. We'd had a hunch, both Waldemar and I, that had slowly condensed into certainty during the conversation, and when the words *Torbi el Mekki, the Healer of Skhirat* were mentioned, it wasn't surprise I felt – only displeasure at this collision with reality. Nor was Waldemar exactly beaming with the kind of land-in-sight thrill one might have imagined.

"Tell about the healer," Waldemar asked Olegsander in his English, which had improved markedly during the trip.

"He's a great man," said Olegsander. "Greater than life and death."

When they stood before one another, Olegsander could sense that God was working through Torbi el Mekki. The healing had consisted of him blessing a bottle of water, which Olegsander then drank.

"What did it taste like?" I asked.

"Like the whole universe," said Olegsander, laughing

happily with his motionless head. His discomfort had been alleviated almost straightaway after drinking it, and today he felt better than he had in years. He couldn't wait to get home to Uncle Bogdan.

Olegsander took a big gulp of his beer. His brother said something to him in Ukrainian, then turned to us:

"Oleg can only drink half a beer, because if he falls over he could die."

"Not anymore," said Olegsander, "not anymore," but his free hand, the one that wasn't pointing straight out to the side, still yielded the beer to his brother, who put it on the table. Olegsander couldn't bend forward far enough to put it there himself. His hand groped for his brother's, and they sat there for a moment holding hands. A tear ran down Sergej's cheek. He wiped it discreetly away with his shoulder.

"Do you remember the last time we played football together?" said Olegsander.

Sergej nodded. He remembered.

"And do you remember we used to fly kites in the thistle field in the autumn? We would run to make them climb? You painted a red sun on yours."

Sergej nodded again. He remembered that too.

"We'll be running again once Uncle Bogdan has taken off the brace. I can feel it in my body."

Then they both cried.

When we got into the van the next day, we had a clearer picture than ever of Torbi el Mekki. We'd said goodbye to Sergej and Olegsander, waving them off as

Olegsander was manoeuvred into the back seat, where he half lay, half sat, and he waved back with his free arm as they drove away down the narrow street between the stacks of tyres.

Waldemar didn't want to talk about it. As we drove I said things like, *Poor Olegsander, he'll die if his uncle removes that brace*, but he brushed me off, saying that nothing had been settled one way or the other by that encounter, that we couldn't know if the water had worked or not.

"Now we know he's still healing people."

"We know he's giving them water to drink."

"Just drive."

Then he sank into himself and had one of his comatose attacks, sitting still for half an hour without a word as we drove. Continuing south.

The desert wasn't what we had imagined. There were no Sahara dunes and yellow sand, just stone and brown crusts with scattered, shaggy bushes. My grumbling about the lack of GPS had now been silenced in favour of a lament over the lack of air conditioning in the van, and over the heat in general. Not that I was suffering all that much with the heat, but during long stretches through the desert Waldemar was too drowsy to really say anything; he wasn't up to much beyond sucking at regular intervals on the water bottles that contained my special blend of water, juice and salt, so I took it upon myself to complain for us both. The bushes were the same colour as the earth. Everything leapt and danced in the flickering air. Scraps of tyre and rubbish lay along the roadside. There was no purity in this desert. This desert was a filthy desert. Everywhere we stopped there was the same sweetish smell of rottenness, of refuse discarded in the sun, of burning waste. We saw the mummified body of a dog baring its teeth, animal and human excrement dried into morsels, an old man pulling his tunic up to his knees and squatting down to piss, a still-living dog being beaten with a piece of rope, whirlwinds arising in the distance like thin brown stems, a sandstorm rolling over a dead world like a fog, the shadows of the bushes, more visible than the bushes themselves, sporadic settlements and people along the road, way stations and cafés selling diarrhoea food, the ever-present Cokes, a black-haired woman stepping out of a doorway and staring furiously at us, a handful of men in a pickup truck, singing and passing around a plastic bottle containing a brown liquid. More brown, encircling our whole field of vision. And ochre and purple. A light like water. It was impossible to draw a straight line: everything melted; there was no sharp horizon. Everything was quenched in light, steeped in it.

Staying overnight in a town whose name I never caught, I had to help Waldemar up to the first floor of the hotel. We went down a corridor that smelled of mould, and since half the door numbers had fallen off I opened the wrong room, where a woman weighing several hundred kilos lay on a divan, staring into space. She'd pulled up her dress to air a turquoise rash on her thigh. On the floor dozed two mangy white cats with bald patches and pointed rat-like heads, and on the ceiling a fan was slowly turning. A cigarette smoked in the ashtray, the only sign that the woman was alive. Then her eyes moved too. I shut the door, hurried away and found our room, helping Waldemar across to the only bed. He tore off his T-shirt and lay down in his shorts, falling asleep instantly, his breath heavy and wheezing. I started picking pubic hairs off my sheet with a piece of toilet paper, then went to throw it in the toilet. I switched on the fan and opened the window in the bathroom. Waldemar was sweating, so I took a towel from our luggage, wetted it in the sink and laid it over his forehead and around his carotid arteries – like the collar of an Eskimo's parka. He opened his eyes. "That helps," he said, and was gone again.

I collapsed onto the bed. Breathing was like inhaling tainted, lukewarm soup. Somewhere outside the window, a donkey was braying like a rusty bellows. A cockroach crossed the floor: swift, scanning jerks, with watchful pauses in between. I lay on my belly and watched it. Gradually I slipped into a confused doze, my defences down, things popping into my head in random order. Suddenly Håkon was enthroned on his mountain in Herning like an evil warlock, then I was sitting in the office, where my talents never really sufficed, then I fell off the bike with Amalie, then I was ten years old myself, and everything was still fresh, not yet at a deadlock: nothing was too late. And so it went on. My whole wasted life piling up in that hotel room like a vast, stinking heap of dung.

In my belly lurked a nasty little parasite that had hopped aboard on our first day in Morocco. It gave me constipation and frantic diarrhoea by turns. I was in a diarrhoea phase, and was thirsty – by now water had started appearing in all the confused scenarios running through my head. Getting up from the bed, I went downstairs and through the foyer, where three men were watching a football match on a little TV. They paid me no attention. The green pitch seemed especially out of place, even on a television screen. I fetched water and juice and salt from the Volkswagen, triple checked that it was locked, then went back up to the room and made two bottles of my aforementioned watery lifeline, my cholera concoction, which consisted of a pinch of salt, a few hundred millilitres of fruit juice and just under a litre of water. I put one bottle by Waldemar's bed and one by my own. Waldemar was talking in his sleep about Torbi el Mekki. He rattled off syndromes and sicknesses, coughed, and then was obviously with his family, muttering abruptly that there was banana in the cake.

Waldemar began the next day with a nosebleed, then fainted onto the hotel-room floor. But once he got down to the van, he claimed he was feeling better than he had in days. Even so, I felt like a murderer as I turned the key in the ignition.

We drove for the rest of the day, taking a long break at a restaurant with air conditioning.

"We're getting close to Skhirat," I said to Waldemar. Waldemar nodded.

At sundown we stopped outside a small town and took a walk to stretch our legs. I always locked the van, even though we weren't going far. Nearby was an abandoned house, half the roof fallen in. On one end hung a sign with a picture of a hen. Sitting down on a little hillock behind the house, we watched the sun setting into the sand.

"Sitting here it seems nuts to think that home can exist at the same time. Feels like hundreds of years since we left Stentofte."

"At least," I said. "Thousands."

A dog came trotting up and started sniffing at Waldemar's shoes. There wasn't much meat on it, all ribs and protruding spine. Its fur looked to be falling out in clumps. The sun grew enormous and fiery red before it disappeared. Then came a fog or a veil gliding across the desert from the horizon, but just as I thought the phenomenon was about to reach us it vanished, and everything was clear in the last light, and the stars began to prick through one by one. The dog grew bolder in the darkness and started gnawing Waldemar's shoes. I picked up a stone, which was enough to make it stop. When I raised my hand with the stone, it ran off to a distance and stood surveying us.

"That's a good trick against dogs," I said. "You don't need to throw the stone – often it's enough just to pick it up and it'll leave you in peace."

"There's another three coming," said Waldemar.

Three dogs that looked like they'd been cast in the same mould as the first had arrived, and stood growling at us. Skinny and dark.

"Did you see where they came from?" I asked Waldemar.

"Ah, they just came walking out of the desert. There's another one," he said, pointing at yet another dog stealing out of the darkness.

"Come on, let's go back to the van."

When we turned around, another two dogs had appeared between us and the van. They drew back their upper lips and bared their teeth as we approached.

"You'd better pick up a stone."

Waldemar picked up a stone.

We tried to walk in an arc around them, but the dogs moved with us, lowering their heads and pointed yellow incisors, blocking the way. The other dogs came closer from behind. They were starting to bark and snap at our trouser legs, and one of them bit my calf. At the same time Waldemar cursed with pain and flung his stone at a dog that had bitten his ankle.

I kicked one of the ones in our way as hard as I could in the stomach, and it rolled onto its back and started howling. That made the others fall back, and we used the opportunity to hurry over to the van. As I got the key out of my pocket and stood bending over the lock, the dogs were on us again: a pair of jaws snapped between my face and the van door, so close I could smell rotten meat, and the key slipped out of my hands. When Waldemar bent down to pick it up, one of the bigger ones leapt out of the pack and snapped at his throat. I saw it coming, a dark shadow out of the corner of my eye, and managed to yank him up by the collar as I felt a mouth close around my calf again. This time the bite was harder; the teeth sank into my skin with a hot pain. I roared. The dog that bit me shrank a few steps back and watched expectantly. The others followed its example. The key lay a foot or two away from the front paws of a dog that was missing one eye and gasping excitedly for breath.

"Leave it," I said. "We'll get onto the roof of the van."

I hauled Waldemar with me up onto the narrow, steep bonnet of the Volkswagen, and at the same time the dogs shot towards us again. They seemed even more demented now, snapping at the empty air and scratching their claws against the paint.

We scrabbled backwards up the windscreen and onto the roof. I broke off one wiper with my foot. The dogs on the ground leapt over one other, baying with white rage.

After we'd been sitting still long enough for Waldemar to catch his breath, they calmed down. Stared up at us, then lay on the ground. One of them got up and tried to make the others howl, but it was ignored. Only when we moved around on the roof did they start to growl.

"I've never seen anything like it," I said, rolling up my trousers to inspect the bites on my calves. On the right one, two teeth had gone in, leaving thin streaks of blood running down the hairy white flesh.

"That doesn't look good," said Waldemar.

"It'll be fine. What about yours?"

Waldemar pulled up his trouser leg. His white tennis sock had spots of blood at the ankle.

"Try to pull your sock down."

Waldemar revealed some wounds that looked like mine, and a load of red marks where the skin had not been broken.

"We could have been bitten much worse," I said.

"Yeah . . . If only we had something to throw at them."

"I've been thinking this whole time we should have brought a weapon on this trip."

"How long do you think they'll stay down there?"

"Absolutely no idea."

Waldemar lay down on his back. I got up and looked down at the keys, which lay in the dust next to the driver's side door. There had been no traffic on the road since we'd been chased onto the roof. It was oddly empty, and we'd also parked so far into the car park that the hut blocked us from view, so we weren't sure we'd be noticed by passers-by. I lay down too and gazed up at the stars.

"There it is, our galaxy," I said.

"Yeah. I've never seen such a starry sky before."

"No, there's too much light in the city at night."

The way I remember it, the stars were different colours. Some were faintly red, others more blue and purple. Spanning the sky was a belt of stars that weren't visible individually, but only as a white veil. The new moon was low.

"It's not the worst place to have a lie down, is it?" said Waldemar.

"No."

"It's so quiet here you can hear your blood."

Waldemar got up and peeped down at the ground. The dogs started growling. "They're still there," he said, lying down.

"There was a shooting star."

"Oh, I didn't see it."

"Just lie down and look."

"Don't they say it gets cold in the desert at night?"

"Yeah, I thought so too, but right now it's just really pleasant."

"Maybe it's not a proper desert?"

"I mean, it looks like a proper desert, as far as I can see."

"A dog desert."

"Yeah."

"Hey, there's one!"

"Bloody amazing."

"They say you're supposed to make a wish, right?"

"Sure, I guess you can. It's a comet burning up in the atmosphere. Wish away."

"I wish for a cap gun."

"Argh, no, you're not supposed to say it."

"Does it not work then?"

"Nah."

"Oh."

"There'll probably be more."

"Yeah."

"Were you figuring a cap gun would just fall from the sky?"

"I don't know. Worth a shot though."

"Pretty tame wish, then."

"It was a test wish. I'm sure we won't be here all night."

And so we lay for ages, alternatively chatting and falling silent, gazing up at the stars. The moon pursued its course across the sky. A car passed on the road, and I stood up on the roof and waved both arms, but it didn't stop. Shortly afterwards another one passed, and the same thing happened. After that there weren't any others. Two dogs began fighting. Their snarls and howling lasted several minutes before calm was restored. Waldemar snored. I sat down by the edge. The dogs had become dark blotches in the shadows. Rolled up carpets, brooding bundles. Were they even there? I crawled down onto the bonnet and put a cautious foot onto the ground, but then the bundles came to life, rushing up with snapping jaws and teeth and eyes that kindled in the dark, and I clambered back onto the roof, and the tumultuous aggression that had suddenly arisen withdrew into itself, reduced to a lurking presence. Motionless, shadowy clumps. But they *were* dogs.

Another light appeared in the desert. It started as a little white haze, and I sat watching it grow larger. When the car drove over a bump, the light was flung up into the sky, and the air blazed for a radius of several kilometres: they had enormous power in the dense darkness of the desert, the headlights. Not visible separately, they remained one melded white light as they approached. The car had the main beams on.

Waldemar, waking, sat up on the roof. The dogs re-emerged from the darkness. They bit at the air, dug in the sand, growled and whined.

Soon the light was so sharp that everything was black and white, and the harsh shadows moved like hands on a clock. Everything not inside the beam was excluded, creating a colourless space of cold light. We could no longer see the stars. Above us was only darkness; the headlights of the car were the only light in the world.

We couldn't figure out what had become of the moon. Where had the moon gone? And above our heads that fidgety dark. "Oh, moon and stars, where have you gone to? And that caustic light approaching, what does that light want? Oh light, light, caustic light, what do you want with us in this crowded darkness? Be not so white and caustic and cold! And darkness, oh darkness, what are you hiding? Answer us, be not so silent and black and vast!"

But there was no answer, only silence. And out of the silence grew the sound of the car's tyres rolling over the worn asphalt and onto the gravel car park, until we were staring straight into the headlights. Then they were lowered; the main beam was switched off. A black shadow sat behind the wheel.

Throughout this whole story I've done my best to be ruthlessly honest, and now I'll admit I was afraid: the shadow behind the wheel made the hair rise all over my body and chilled my skin. But in the fear department Waldemar was a step beyond me – he wasn't afraid, he was petrified. For him, time was no longer dimensional. There was only the terrifying present, with no concept of rescue or escape. The terrifying present, in which he stared, paralysed, straight into the eyes of the ghastly shadow. "Oh, figure at the wheel, what do you want with us in this barren desert? Why do you come tonight, what have we done? Go, go, we shall not die."

The light went out and the engine stopped, and we sat in utter silence on the roof. Once the quiet had settled, the door opened and he climbed out. He walked around the Volkswagen and inhaled the night air, kicked at one of the tyres, looked up at us and laughed his hoarse, cold laughter, while the dogs withdrew into the desert, backwards, bellies against the sand. Then with swift steps he went back to the Audi, opened the door and got behind the wheel. The engine started and the lights were switched back on, casting everything white, and in the piercing whiteness we heard the car turn in the gravel and drive away. Slowly our vision returned as it vanished into the great breaking waves of darkness.

We got to Skhirat in the noontime heat of the following day. A handful of white houses scattered randomly in the desert, as though someone had dropped them. A main road of asphalt running through it, earthen tracks branching off.

We stopped at a little kiosk, a hole in the wall beneath a lopsided awning, and the man pointed. Straight ahead, he lived outside of town. We would see it.

The town petered out, and ahead we saw a house to the right of the road, set a few hundred metres back. A gravel track led from the tarmac to the house, and along the track were several parked cars. We parked and took out the wheelchair, then walked the last hundred metres. All around the low house with its flat roof, junk was heaped against the walls. Sticks were poking out of the surrounding desert sands. It looked like people had been buried there. All was silent. The sun was at its zenith in the sky, and there were no shadows. A lizard bolted across the road and underneath a bush. A bell rang inside the house. Afterwards a woman emerged from the black doorway. One half of her face was covered by a doughy tumour, and judging by the size of the scarf she was wearing it extended over most of her head as well. Scattered wiry hairs were growing out of it, as on a fly. She carried a bottle of water in her hand. Her family was waiting outside.

To one side was a booth beneath a parasol. There was a queue of pilgrims at the booth. The first of them moved with ceremonial slowness from the queue into the house.

It wasn't a graveyard. The sticks poking out of the ground were crutches, a whole forest of them. They pointed out of the earth at odd angles, each casting a short shadow. There were modern crutches made of metal, with arm pads and plastic handles, and wooden crutches with a cross-piece at the top designed for the armpit. Smaller canes, some wooden with a curved handle, and other finer, black ones with carved heads. Some of them just looked like sticks people had used to support themselves for lack of a better option. They stood in pairs and individually. The junk consisted of wheelchairs stacked against the wall. One of them stood a little apart from the others, and it looked to be over a hundred years old. The mouldering tyres had fallen off the wheels and lay in two circles in the dust. On the seat was a prosthetic leg, the skin-coloured paint peeling off in ribbons to reveal the wood underneath.

We went to the back of the queue. The bell rang

again, and a pilgrim came out through the doorway, and another moved from the queue to the door and went inside. In front of us was an Asian couple. The man was holding an umbrella to shield his wife from the sun. It was an impressive piece of foresight. The bell rang again, and again the queue moved. Soon we were under the shadow of the parasol. Waldemar was dozing in his wheelchair, and I shook him. The man beneath the parasol was selling bottles of water to those seeking a cure. The bell rang. A pilgrim emerged from the doorway with his bottle of water, and a woman carrying an infant went inside. It hadn't made a noise in all the time we'd been standing in the queue. No one said a word; everything proceeded in silence. It was the Asian couple's turn now. The man folded his umbrella and they bought a bottle of water. The bell rang. The infant was carried out. They walked towards the door, she supporting herself on his arm. They hesitated before stepping into the shadow. The man beneath the parasol, the last human we met before Torbi el Mekki, sold us our spring water.

When the bell rang, I started feeling dizzy. It was like some dreadful exam in a subject that surpassed all understanding – no, it was even worse. I felt like I was about to be executed. I was about to throw up. The water was lying in Waldemar's lap. I staggered after him. For a moment my vision failed and everything went white, and it felt as though something hit me in the solar plexus. The blow struck right beneath my ribs. There was a deep bass note of pain and I crumpled forwards, but when I could see again no one was there. Waldemar had stopped outside the door. I caught up with him in a chaos of pain, light, nausea and sweat, and we went together into the darkness. I was right behind him.

I tried opening my eyes to see, but couldn't; but then I did see him, and it struck me that I'd had my eyes open the whole time, but that he only slowly took shape in the massive darkness of the shuttered room. He took his time emerging.

He was gigantic. He sat on a carpet in a tunic, eyes cast to the ground, running a hand over his bald head in a pensive gesture. There might have been people watching us from the corners without us knowing, it was so dark, but in the middle of the room where he sat a crack of light from the doorway made it inside. He looked up at Waldemar, rose and took the water, then sat down again. The silence had been colossal and lasted an age, but now he was intoning something in Arabic, his head bowed over the water in his hands. I felt tremendous hatred. That was all I felt. I wanted to kick him. Then he rose for a second time, nodded at Waldemar and handed him the water. He went across to the bell. I saw it glint in the dark. It rang as we left the house.

We returned to the Volkswagen, the bottle back in Waldemar's lap. The Asian couple sat in their car with the engine running. She drank the last of her water and screwed the top back onto the empty bottle, while he watched her with his hands resting on the wheel. She looked at him, and he began to cry.

When I started the van and drove out onto the asphalt road, I should have turned back to Skhirat, but instead I turned the opposite way and continued south. Waldemar still had his stupid water in his lap, and was peering at the dancing stems of dust further into the desert. They seemed as thin as pencils. I drove for the rest of the day without any clue what I should say to him. I drove slowly. A lorry overtook us, flinging a stone up against the windscreen. There was a little bang and a little star. Neither of us reacted. To the west, the sun was going down in a cloud of sand that coloured the light orange. The desert was still dotted with bushes, but they thinned out as we carried on. We drove all night. At some point I fell asleep, waking when the right-side wheels crunched in the gravel on the verge. I slowed down, got back onto the road and continued. Waldemar still hadn't said a word, but I think he was awake. The starry sky reached all the way to the horizon, visible through the windscreen until the light came and plucked it away. It was morning, and we were still silent.

I pulled over to stretch my legs. The sun had broken free of the horizon and was beginning to warm the ground. There were no longer grey bushes in the desert, only cracked earth and sand. Waldemar got out too, the water still in his hand, and sat on the tarmac with his feet on the verge. This early in the morning, the tarmac wasn't fluid yet. He cast a long, heavy shadow away from the road.

"That water's starting to get on my nerves," I said.

"Yeah, mine too," said Waldemar. Then he unscrewed the top and tipped the bottle carefully, so that the water poured in one long and glittering jet onto the ground. It formed a little stream that trickled quite a way into the desert before it was sucked up by the earth, which was so dry it struggled to drink. Leaving a dark line that pointed west.

I stood behind him and to one side, watching everything with the sun at my back. I felt both relief and dismay. Relief because the final indignity of drinking the water would have been too much for me. The water was a flowing mockery of Waldemar and his illnesses. Yet I think Waldemar himself was indifferent. He did it for my sake. He was hardened, and could easily have managed it, could have drunk the water and confirmed that it was only water, at once completely magical and utterly profane.

But at the same time, I felt dismay, because it was such a definitive act: it was clear, now, that this was over. Waldemar's nose was bleeding. A little red streak appeared beneath one nostril, running straight down until it reached the cautious curve of the lip then probing for the corner of the mouth. For a moment I was unsure if it might not have been a colossal mistake, pouring out the water. The same way you can refuse to walk under a ladder or worry about breaking a mirror, even though you know that a broken mirror is nothing but a broken mirror and a ladder is just a ladder. And I twitched as I suppressed the impulse to run over and scoop up the wet sand in an attempt to save the water. But I just stood there. For ages. The sense of being present changed, becoming a drunken optical illusion in which various things bulged and came into special focus as though they were taking turns stepping into the centre of a surveillance mirror. The water bottle Waldemar held in his hands was suddenly deadly clear. I got the sense I was sleeping, and somewhere beyond sleep in a waking world there was someone calling my name, but as yet the voices hadn't made themselves manifest here as anything but a vanguard of indeterminate unease, constantly on the verge of reality and breaking through. We couldn't possibly be in Morocco. I put my hand on the Volkswagen's burning paint to support myself. The desert was a requiem of sand and sun. I stared into the air, which grew hotter and hotter, and while I gazed the redness of the landscape gained in strength, and for a moment I thought I might be on Mars. Yes, Mars. A mute and lifeless place with the vague promise of frozen water and the hope of an atmosphere, but otherwise just red dust, red on red. Red and dead. The sun rose in mechanical jerks. Gradually the whole place became animated. A red liquid trickled up out of the sand, and soon it was obvious it was blood, and I don't know how much time passed before rivers appeared, sluggish-flowing and muddy as though flooded, and they carried refuse and burning car tyres.

Down the road a regiment came marching, slow-moving and hazy in the air, which flickered and danced in layers like petrol and water. It was an army on retreat, that was obvious, I thought at that point, but as they approached I saw they were macaques, their grey fur caked in dust, and what I had thought were rifles and bayonets turned out to be rolling stands with bags containing a clear liquid, and from the bags there were tubes that ended in their arms.

We both sat watching as they passed in total silence. The sun was high now, and the asphalt had started to melt in the scouring light.

"What are we going to do?" I asked. I felt completely helpless and alone, and couldn't bring myself to talk about the water. I couldn't even say the word.

"Is there anything you need to do back home?" asked Waldemar.

"No."

"Then let's just keep going south."

"There's no point."

"You've been saying that since day one."

I gazed across the flat expanse, earthen desert filling

every inch of my field of vision. It was like an enormous hotplate.

After a while Waldemar said, "I heard about a healer in South Africa, I thought we could drive down there and pay him a visit. Apparently you drink an enchanted Coke."

Both of us laughed.

I don't know what kind of dread made me go along with Waldemar's silly idea of continuing south, but I helped him back into the van and we kept going. I felt a deep sense of guilt, as though somehow I was responsible for the healer's actions, and while I drove stuff kept popping out of the heat and disappearing again. I saw a thudding heart in an oven. A laughing monkey, its eye sockets giving birth to yellow budgies. They rose aloft like small fluttering plague flags hoisted above a sea of photons and boiling sand. The steering wheel quivered and trembled in my hands, as though in the throes of a death that wouldn't stop. I drove and drove and drove. Waldemar was quiet again. The sun was high, and nothing cast a shadow. It was impossible to keep track of time. There's a gap here where I remember nothing, but then I do remember looking up from the road and seeing that we were in a real desert, the kind we'd wished for, not the dirty, dusty, bushy semi-desert we'd battled through but a true desert of naked sand, of absolute purity.

The first time I saw Waldemar walk any significant distance was when his wheelchair died after Martha's funeral, and the second time was when we climbed an enormous sand dune that grew out of the road and into the desert. He was breathing like his lungs were filled with sand. At the top he was satisfied, and when he'd got his breath back enough to speak he said it was a proper desert, this, and we sat gazing west, away from the road. Somewhere out there was the Atlantic, puffing oxygen, but all we saw was burning sand. I wondered whether we'd reached Western Sahara. I had no idea where we were or how long we'd been driving. I hadn't slept since the night before we visited the healer. Had we taken our passports out? Had we crossed a border? We were in Africa, that much I knew, and Waldemar was alive; in Africa, and Waldemar was alive and writing his name in the sand with a finger.

We took off our shoes and socks and buried our feet. Under the blazing surface it was relatively cool. A bone-dry ocean stretched before us, and the wind moved the grains of sand from crest to crest, whistling with such depth it was as though we heard the planet itself tumbling through empty space.

There were no animals or flora, only sand. No shadows, only sun. Our only company in the monstrous shimmering were the desert mosquitoes, which were a different, soundless type of mosquito, darker and more frail, and their proboscises delivered a spiced little pain that lasted weeks. Sand and wind were the two factors that shaped the landscape. It consisted of dunes with one soft side on a gentle slant and a harder, steeper side that appeared faintly concave. A play of concave and convex surfaces, of hollows and peaks. There was crêpey sand, washboard sand and entirely flat sand. Sand whose surface was a porous shell above an underlying softness, and sand which on top was more liquid than water, and whose viscosity increased the further you sank. The wind played continually with the sand, heaping it into piles and sorting it according to grain size, arranging it into shapes at whim. The wind had time on its side. And the sun beat the sand with near-audible intensity. All fat and nourishment and liquid were burned away. The desert was a giant pool of sun, a giant playground for the light and the killing heat, a cabinet of mirrors in which judging distance was impossible and all sense of time gone, and the only clock was the slow desiccation into death.

A beetle emerged from a hole in the sand and started crawling against the wind. "Look," I said to Waldemar. It was about as surprising as if a pattern of frost had bloomed. The beetle held its hind parts aloft as it crawled, as though keen to avoid burning its belly on the sand, and the six legs left a little symphony of dents with their Morse code-like tap-tap-tapping. Its shell was matt and dark. The movements of its legs somehow emphasised its beetly silence; there was something at once determined and hesitant about it, like a constant waking from a dream weighted with meaning. For the beetle, the world was sand. We stared at it so long it became a mastodon.

Then we were back in the van and driving. Ahead there was a lighthouse of black smoke, which we'd been heading towards for hours. As we got closer, we saw a petrol station. A man in a faded blue tunic was burning a pile of tyres, poking at them with an iron rod and trying to lift them back into place so they would burn better. The flames were invisible in the heat, but the smoke rose so thick and tall that it looked like a column of night. When we looked at him, he looked away. We filled up and paid without a word exchanged. I'm not sure the man serving us even had a mouth. It appeared to be overgrown by knotted scar tissue. Flies crawled across his face, and he didn't seem to notice.

Back in the van, I started talking again. Waldemar didn't say much. I asked about his family, and his answer was evasive and nonsensical. At some point he asked where we were. He had no idea, and I was alarmed. The black smoke was visible in the rear-view mirror long afterwards, a diffuse threat as we drove down the winding road. The sand drifted across the dark, pitted asphalt as though that was better than being on the other side. It evoked memories of a Teflon pan of sugar being shaken. Tiredness was prompting strange connections. The burning tyres became a heap of eels devouring one another, and I must have been driving in my sleep for a while because I woke to find the wheel in my hands and Waldemar coughing. Despite the scalding sun he was noticeably pale, almost greenish. The sun was setting for the umpteenth time. And with the shattering sunlight out of my head there appeared a series of clear thoughts, as though cogency were something that belonged to the night. And the train of thought ended with me slowing the van and turning around and heading north – motivated by the panicky fear that Waldemar would die here in the desert. It would be a terrible crime. He had to go home to his family. I stepped on the accelerator, driving as fast as I could, but after I'd been driving some time it occurred to me that there wasn't time enough to reach home, that there wasn't even time to reach the nearest town, where I could hand over Waldemar to someone who might take responsibility, so I turned around once more, slowing down and driving south again. How long could the desert last? There had to be a town soon; my best chance was to carry on south. Then I remembered it was ages since either one of us had drunk anything, so I pulled over and went round the back and made a bottle of my cholera concoction, spilling salt all over the floor, then came back round and gave Waldemar the bottle. He took it with both hands and put it in his lap without drinking. I helped the bottle to his lips and tilted up the base; most of it ran down his front, but I think he got some down, and then he coughed again, and a blob of sticky mucous flew onto the door of the glove compartment. I apologised for getting us into this nightmare and tried to make him drink more, and then he said something; I could only catch the word *Mum*, and it made me break into strange sobs and start the van and yank it around in a panicked version of a three-point turn that got the wheels stuck in the sand, where they whined and whirred while I did everything wrong and dug them deeper and deeper, until suddenly they gained purchase and I got back up onto the road, exultant and shouting, *It's working again!* But it only lasted a brief moment. Then the fear was back, grinding and gnawing, and I tried to remember how long we'd been driving, how many days had passed since Skhirat. The whole thing condensed abruptly into violent hatred of Torbi el Mekki and of Denmark, and I sat shouting and screaming curses into the air.

"Ah, shut up," mumbled Waldemar.

A huge relief! I was glad to hear him say something sensible – it had been so long.

"I'm driving you back to Skhirat," I told him. "Just hang on, we'll be in Skhirat soon," but Waldemar seemed to panic at the thought of going back to Skhirat and kept moaning, *No.* I insisted we continue, and he undid his seatbelt and tried to open the door and climb out. I grabbed his T-shirt and braked and got the door shut. But when I started driving again, he lunged at the wheel and I had to slam on the brakes. I don't know if it was his sense of consequence asserting itself, or if it was his stubbornness: he'd taken a decision to move ceaselessly south and was keeping that firmly in his mind. Would he prefer not to return to the defeat of our visit to the healer? Did he even think it was a defeat? Personally, every now and then, I think of it as a victory. It was a victory driving clear across a third of the globe for a bottle of water, and when it was obtained, pouring it out. That was Waldemar's opinion on the whole thing. That it should be poured into the sand. Maybe the trip was a great victory and a great tragedy? And maybe, since he could tell it was all over anyway, he didn't want to make the final concession of turning around and driving back? I don't know how considered it was, because after he'd asked me to shut up and tried to get out mid-journey and grabbed the wheel, he fell back into his comatose state. Maybe his brain was affected by one of his diseases, in which case what I did was even less defensible than if he'd been in his right mind, and even then it couldn't be defended: I turned the van around and drove back south. My excuse was to tell myself it was bound to be the shortest way to a hospital. But in the sun-baked stew of my sandy brain, I was stalked by the nightmarishly clear certainty that the road had curled into a Möbius strip, and that we were driving along an unending ribbon of black asphalt at night, and that the whole world outside had vanished. For a while that was all I could think, and then new thoughts came, new horrifying scenarios, and the night was so long that every single sick little thought had an eternity in which to unfurl. I kept listening to Waldemar's breathing. His breathing and my driving were all that existed. Now and again he stopped, then came back with a kind of rattling snore. At some point it struck me that his breathing was bound up with the pressure of my foot on the accelerator, and the condition of his organs with the hands on the dashboard. These murky connections and causalities haunted me constantly. I started talking to him, and once I'd started I couldn't stop. I kept talking, because if I fell silent it was like the road tipped and we were driving upside down, driving on the underside of the globe, and the illusion of up and down was revoked. I chatted about my childhood, telling anecdotes, talking about girls I'd known. And if I paused for a moment to think or try to recall something, we tipped around and hung heads downwards in a vast darkness, and I had to bite my lip or slap myself and start talking again simply to establish what was up and what was down. I took off one shoe, hoping the difference in temperature between my feet would keep me awake. Put the fan on full blast, straight into my face. Rolled the window up and down. Sang occasionally, when I couldn't think of anything to say. If only I could keep myself awake and driving south, Waldemar would stay alive. I believed that with the conviction of a child believing he mustn't step on the cracks. There were periods when I had a strong urge to pull over and take a dip in a sea in the darkness. I could hear the waves, and I had to say out loud that we were driving through a desert, and then I sat there and sang: "D-E-S means DES, E-R-T means ERT, means DES, means ERT means DESERT," and then a stretch of time would pass in which we were driving through a desert, and then the impulse to stop and throw off my clothes and run naked into the waves came back. I could hear it simmering, mild and summery and Scandinavian, could hear the smooching tongues of the waves and the sand. "D-E-S," I began, as though we were two shitty boy scouts on a trip. "Come on, Waldemar, D-E-S means . . ." But Waldemar was silent. I shook him, and he raised his head enough to look me in the eyes, and his gaze was so oddly clear that it felt like looking at a snowflake through a microscope. Then a car appeared behind us. It had its main beams on, creating a halo in the desert. Waldemar's chin dropped to his chest. The seatbelt kept him upright. The black Audi overtook us and vanished without a sound. The two red tail lights stared back at me.

Pulling over onto the verge, I undid Waldemar's seatbelt and held him. I think I sobbed. I can't remember anything for sure. It was night time, that I know. I tried once more to get Waldemar to drink something, but it ran out of his mouth and he fell limply into my lap. I didn't have the strength to lift my arms and start the van; I hadn't got a clue which way to go. I was never sure whether I was asleep or awake. Whether a moment had passed since the last thought or if I'd been asleep in the meantime. At some point Waldemar's body stiffened, and I sat him back up in the seat as well as I could. Horror took turns with a strange, resigned calm. Did I speak to him? I could see the stars outside. I kept jumping because I thought a car was coming, but no car came. In the end I must have lost consciousness.

I woke up in a hospital that smelled of death and chemicals and hummed with a language I didn't understand. I had a saline drip in my arm, and in the bed next to me was an old man whose belly was so swollen he couldn't wear a hospital gown: it was unbuttoned from the chest down, revealing the bloated, shiny skin. I began to shout. A nurse appeared. She shushed me, and the man with the swollen belly turned his head and looked and turned it back towards the window. The glass was dazzling with sun. I could see nothing outside but a whiteness that seared my eyes.

Later, at a police station, I sat opposite two officers and was questioned. I remember it was light when I arrived and grew dark as I sat there. The office was as cold as a fridge with the air conditioning. Finally, they let me out onto the street. I bought a Coke from a hawker who fished it out of a cooler filled with brown water. I sat down on a step and drank. My hair was greasy, and my scalp itched. My beard had grown too long and was itchy too. Waldemar must still be in hospital; I'd asked about him, and the doctor had pointed at the floor. Then the police had fetched me. I walked back to the hospital. For twenty-four hours I waited in a waiting room, sleeping on a chair. Enquiring now and then at a desk. At last I was handed a piece of paper. It was a death certificate.

And only now, with this piece of paper, it was as if things became real, that I could act. I visited the Danish consulate and they contacted Waldemar's family. I didn't dare do it myself; I tried, but had to give up with the telephone in my hand, passing it back to one of the consulate staff as my lips quivered.

And with the death certificate Waldemar was captured by a world which for a while we had escaped. First and foremost, an absolute inflexibility reasserted itself, dictated by bureaucratic and financial problems. Although with every bite of food we eat and every breath we take we assimilate those who have died before us, and so in death, gradually, we spread across a greater area and become more mobile than we ever were in life, a corpse has virtually no freedom of movement – not until by rotting and being incorporated into a wider cycle it has escaped culture. The only rational thing would have been to drive Waldemar home in the Volkswagen, but Waldemar was taboo, so I couldn't just drive him home in the Volkswagen. The dead don't drive Volkswagens. Waldemar had felt for most of his life like he was a burden, and it was now as though in death, because of his aforementioned sense of consequence and his enormous stubbornness, he had decided to persist in being one. He had freed himself completely, and only reluctantly allowed himself to be trapped by coffins and undertakers and customs officers and forms and gravestones. Only reluctantly allowed himself to be sucked back up to Denmark.

I remember things like a corpse passport. I remember that Waldemar didn't need to have a corpse passport if he was going to be burned and transported in an urn, but that he would need one if transported in a coffin. Waldemar's family wanted to see him one last time, and the authorities wanted to do an autopsy, so Waldemar had to go home in a coffin. The rest of the money from the Monte Carlo Casino covered the expense of a particularly thick and solid travelling coffin and transportation home.

In the evening I collapsed into bed in a hotel room. I fell asleep instantly, but woke every half hour all night long from nightmares about bureaucracy and death and deserts. I stared into the darkness with no clue where I was, and once or twice I thought the whole thing had been a dream, that I was still working at the office, and that Sara was beside me, and for several seconds a great stream of relief rushed through me, before consciousness properly returned and the horror was that much worse.

The Volkswagen I left down there with the key in the ignition, and we took the same plane home. I had Waldemar's corpse passport and his regular passport and other documents in my hand luggage, and we got to customs in Denmark, and there the police took over. They were waiting for me, making an encounter with Waldemar's family impossible.

Waldemar was autopsied, and they determined he had died what's called a natural death. He was buried on a Sunday, and I didn't go to Stentofte for the funeral, sitting instead in my flat in Sydhavnen with the TV on, to make the silence come to life. I watched the news. They were almost finished building that mountain in Herning. Right now it looked like a big pile of earth and granite, but soon it would start to grow plants. Håkon appeared onscreen, and I switched it off. I decided to use the last of my money on going out to eat. I couldn't bear sitting at home.

I chose a fancy restaurant in the centre of town. The waiter presented the food. As usual, I didn't listen. When he was finished I put the fork in the meat, cut off a bite and raised it to my mouth, and chewed. It was as though I was eating Waldemar.

GLOSSARY

Bagger, Stein (p. 107) – Danish convicted criminal and a former entrepreneur.

Fogh (p. 135) – Anders Fogh Rasmussen, Danish Prime Minister, 2001–2009.

PARTHIAN TRANSLATIONS

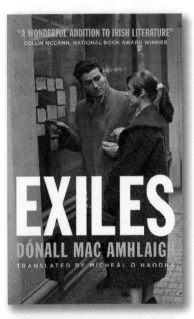

EXILES

Dónall Mac Amhlaigh

Translated from Irish
by Mícheál Ó hAodha

Out October 2020

£12.00
978-1-912681-31-0

HANA

Alena Mornštajnová

Translated from Czech
by Julia and Peter Sherwood

Out October 2020

£10.99
978-1-912681-50-1

Creative
Europe

La Blanche
Maï-Do Hamisultane

LA BLANCHE
Maï-Do Hamisultane

Translated from French
by Suzy Ceulan Hughes

£8.99
978-1-912681-23-5

THE NIGHT CIRCUS
AND OTHER STORIES
Uršuľa Kovalyk

Translated from Slovak
by Julia and Peter Sherwood

£8.99
978-1-912681-04-4

The Night Circus
and Other Stories
Uršuľa Kovalyk

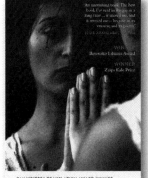

A Glass Eye
Miren Agur Meabe

A GLASS EYE
Miren Agur Meabe

Translated from Basque
by Amaia Gabantxo

£8.99
978-1-912109-54-8

PARTHIAN TRANSLATIONS

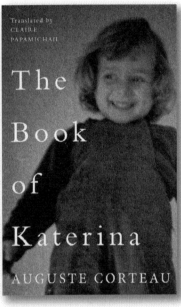

THE BOOK OF KATERINA

Auguste Corteau

Translated from Greek by Claire Papamichail

Out 2021

£10.00
978-1-912681-26-6

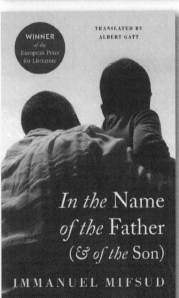

IN THE NAME OF THE FATHER (& OF THE SON)

Immanuel Mifsud

Translated from Maltese by Albert Gatt

£6.99
978-1-912681-30-3

Creative Europe

HER MOTHER'S HANDS

Karmele Jaio

Translated from Basque
by Kristin Addis

£8.99
978-1-912109-55-5

WOMEN WHO BLOW ON KNOTS

Ece Temelkuran

Translated from Turkish
by Alexander Dawe

£9.99
978-1-910901-69-4

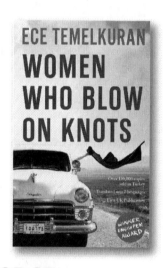

THE HOUSE OF THE DEAF MAN

Peter Krištúfek

Translated from Slovak
by Julia and Peter Sherwood

£11.99
978-1-909844-27-8

Creative Europe

PARTHIAN TRANSLATIONS

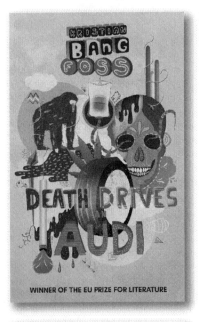

DEATH DRIVES AN AUDI

Kristian Bang Foss

Winner of the European Prize
for Literature

£10.00
978-1-912681-32-7

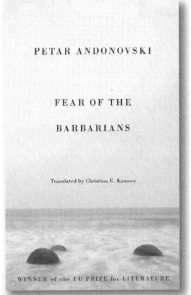

FEAR OF BARBARIANS

Petar Adonovski

Winner of the European Prize
for Literature

£9.00
978-1-913640-19-4

Creative Europe

PARTHIAN TRANSLATIONS

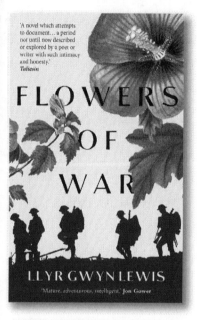

FLOWERS OF WAR

Llyr Gwyn Lewis

Short-Listed for Wales
Book of the Year

£9.00
978-1-912681-25-9

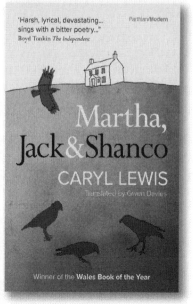

MARTHA, JACK AND SHANCO

Caryl Lewis

Winner of the Wales
Book of the Year

Out October 2020

£9.99
978-1-912681-77-8

Creative
Europe